Sunshine picklelime

Sunshine picklelime

by **Pamela Ellen Ferguson**

illustrated by
Christian Slade

Random House New York

To all the beloved younger members of the Ferguson,
Pearce, and Coombe clans, spread around the world from
the USA to Britain, from Lithuania to Singapore, and from
South Africa to New Zealand. And to the younger members
of the Winiker clan in Switzerland.
—P.E.F.

Text copyright © 2010 by Pamela Ellen Ferguson
Illustrations copyright © 2010 by Christian Slade

All rights reserved. Published in the United States by Random House Children's Books, a division of Random House, Inc., New York.

Random House and the colophon are registered trademarks of Random House, Inc.

Visit us on the Web! www.randomhouse.com/kids

Educators and librarians, for a variety of teaching tools, visit us at www.randomhouse.com/teachers

Library of Congress Cataloging-in-Publication Data
Ferguson, Pamela.
Sunshine Picklelime / by Pamela Ellen Ferguson ; illustrated by Christian Slade. — 1st ed.
p. cm.
Summary: PJ Picklelime can talk to birds, hear bells ringing in a woman's curls, and spot moonbows in the night sky, but when a close friend dies and her parents separate, she searches for understanding and a way to recover her sunshine.
ISBN 978-0-375-86175-8 (trade) — ISBN 978-0-375-96175-5 (lib. bdg.) — ISBN 978-0-375-86174-1 (pbk.) — ISBN 978-0-375-89303-2 (e-book)
[1. Human-animal communication—Fiction. 2. Birds—Fiction. 3. Wildlife rescue—Fiction. 4. Divorce—Fiction. 5. Death—Fiction.] I. Slade, Christian, ill. II. Title.
PZ7.F3569Su 2010
[Fic]—dc22
2009027877

Printed in the United States of America
10 9 8 7 6 5 4 3 2 1

First Edition

Random House Children's Books supports the First Amendment and celebrates the right to read.

CONTENTS

picklelime and lemon pie

PJ Picklelime lives in a village very close to you. Meadows are knee-deep in wildflowers in early springtime. Summers are hot and dreamy when golden peaches the size of melons hang from the trees. Snow drifts like powdered sugar down the mountainside in winter.

PJ lives in a cottage with stone walls and stone floors that keep the family Picklelime cool in the summer and slowly absorb warmth from the sun to keep the family cozy in winter. The Picklelimes have barrels outside to catch rainwater in spring, summer, and autumn and snow in winter. A barrel on the roof pipes sun-heated water directly down into the shower below.

Families from all over the world live in PJ's village because a computer company on the other side of the mountain brought people in from Africa, the Middle East, Asia, Europe, and North America.

PJ looks different from other kids, as she was born with a crop of thick, black curly hair, inherited from the darker side of her mother's family. "Oh, she'll lose that," said neighbor Shanti Patel over the fence one day. But PJ never lost her hair, and it continued to grow each year like a wild bush around her head, even wilder when winds heavy with salt came off the nearby ocean. Every time her parents tried to cut it, PJ covered her hair with her hands and screamed out loud until they put down the scissors.

"PJ, no one can see who you are under all that hair!" said her mom.

"Think of the money we could get if we sold PJ's hair to the pillow makers," said her dad.

PJ clapped her hands to her ears so their words just sounded all muffled and marshmallowy. "My hair has a job," she insisted. "You don't understand. My hair has work to do." She wouldn't tell her parents exactly what that work was.

You see, one day she had found a tiny little bird, a yellow warbler, peeking unhappily between the branches of the yellow Lady Banks rosebush that had burst into bloom to fill an entire corner of their back garden.

"Why do you look so sad, little friend?" PJ asked, stroking the bird's yellow breast, which was a shade creamier than the roses that clustered around it.

"Because I can't warble," cheeped the bird. "Listen to my silly voice. All the other warblers left me behind when they flew south. They said I couldn't be a warbler because I couldn't warble, so I had to find my own way. But I don't know where to go!"

"I have plenty of space for you," said PJ. She made sure her parents weren't watching from the kitchen window, then she bent over and parted her hair to make room for the tiny bird.

But the bird hesitated. "I've never lived in hair before, only a nest made of twigs and branches and old string and wool and bits of this and bits of that."

"Well, let's say my hair is a new kind of nest, ready-made and waiting for you to move in. You don't even have to pay rent," PJ told the bird.

So the little bird hopped off the branch of the bush and landed in PJ's hair. PJ let go of her curls and they sprang around the warbler protectively, thick enough and black enough to hide his yellow feathers.

"This *is* different," said the bird. "Soft and springy! I think I'm going to like this!"

"Just one problem," said PJ.

"What's that?" cheeped the bird. He dipped his head to burrow through PJ's curls.

"There's no bathroom on board. You'll have to fly in and out. Make sure it's when we're alone and before you go to sleep. If my parents see you, they'll make you go away. This is our secret, OK?"

"OK. Done!" said the bird.

"Now, the next thing we need to work on is your voice," said PJ.

"My voice?" cried the little bird. "But I don't have one. That's why the others left me behind!"

"Nonsense," said PJ. "They were just too impatient. Would you like me to teach you how to sing?"

"How can you? You're not a warbler!"

"No, but I know how to sing!" PJ said.

"Well . . . ," said the little bird.

"Then let's get started." PJ didn't want to waste any time. "Now, you have to fly back into the roses while we work. I can't talk to you when you're buried in my hair since I can't see you or hear you properly."

With a tiny flutter of wings, the little bird untangled

himself from PJ's curls and flew into a cluster of roses a few inches from her nose.

"Perfect." PJ smiled. "You match the flowers! No one can see you except me. OK, first things first. What's your name?"

"I don't know. I'm just the yellow warbler who can't warble," said the bird.

"Hmmm." PJ thought for a moment. "What name would you like?"

"Something sweet?" asked the bird.

"Lemon Pie?" PJ suggested.

The little bird giggled so much, roses bounced around him.

"Right, Lemon Pie it is. Now then, Lemon Pie, let's start with your breath. Don't think about your voice. Just your breath. Breathe in, two, three, pause, then breathe out, two, three. Let's try that together. Breathe in, two, three, pause, and breathe out, two, three. Wasn't that easy?"

"Not easy. Dreamy. I'll fall off my branch if you go on like this!"

"Then snuggle against the petals so you feel safe. Let's try that again, but this time, add a little humming sound. Keep your beak shut and *hummmmmmmm. . . .*"

"Huu, hum, hum, hum, cough cough, huuuuuuuu . . ."

"Beak shut, Lemon Pie. Try to turn *huuuuu* into *huuummmmmm.*"

"Huuu-u-u-mmm."

"There, you see, breath becomes hum!"

"It makes my chest feel all warm."

Each day for several days, PJ and Lemon Pie went to the rosebush after PJ got home from school to *humm* and *aaaah* and *ooooo* and *eeeee* and *ayyyy* at one another, until the bird sort of lost himself in sound and forgot that he didn't know how to sing. But this wasn't really singing. It was a way of practicing different sounds and having fun.

Sometimes at night, Lemon Pie stayed out late and practiced alone under the twinkling stars before flying through PJ's open window to snuggle into her hair against the pillow to sleep.

PJ's mom would stand by the kitchen window and say, "That's an odd-sounding bird out there."

"It isn't a bird," said PJ's dad. "It's a baby raccoon."

Mrs. Patel, their neighbor across the road, thought it was an owl. PJ's art teacher, Pablo dos Santos y Sanchez, who lived on the next block, said it sounded like a young dove. Mr. Splitzky, who lived behind the Picklelimes, said, "It's a singing rosebush!" Blossom, his dog, kept scratching at the corner of the fence where the yellow rose branches draped down gracefully onto his lawn.

Nobody could ever spot Lemon Pie in the clusters of yellow petals. When he wasn't there, he was tucked inside PJ's curls, which grew even bushier to hide him as he grew bigger through the days of springtime.

"Next time ocean winds blow in from the south, they'll whisk you into the sky if you don't let us cut your hair," said PJ's dad.

"But if I get whisked into the sky, my hair will be like a parachute. You'll see me floating and swaying down into the garden," said PJ.

Her mom laughed, but her dad said, "*Don't* encourage her, Maura," and shook his head.

One morning an oil tanker broke up along the nearby coast and hundreds of seabirds and pelicans struggled to survive. Oil covered them and the waves like a huge carpet, black as night. An immediate appeal went out to all the local haircutters and barbers in the area to bag up everything they swept off the floor to help soak up the oil slick.

PJ's parents took her aside and explained the situation and said everyone with long hair was running to the local barber for a quick cut.

"PJ, the community needs your hair," said her mom. "The seabirds need your hair. The waves need your hair. We could fill an *entire* bag just with your mop of curls!"

PJ stood there in silence and asked if she could have a few moments outside to think. Feeling even more protective of the little bird nesting in her dark curls, she walked into the back garden to talk to Lemon Pie near their favorite rosebush. Lemon Pie sat quietly listening to the news, then untangled himself from PJ's hair and hopped onto a branch to be at eye level with her.

"What should we do, Lemon Pie?" PJ asked, cupping her hands around his body. "I can't throw you out, and we haven't finished your singing lessons yet!"

Gentle sea breezes began to stir the branches under Lemon Pie. After a few moments, he said, "I'm growing too big to be hidden by your hair for much longer, PJ. We both know that. You've taught me a new way to sing. The warblers might not recognize my voice, but who cares about them? Perhaps it's time I flew down to the coast to help rescue the seabirds and their eggs. And maybe it's time you cut your hair. Don't worry, it will grow back very quickly. Something else will nest in there. You wait and see!"

And with that, Lemon Pie began to *caw-caw-caw* like a laughing gull and move his wings. PJ opened her hands. He lifted off into the sky, circling a fond farewell above her head, before turning and flying off toward the damaged coast.

CHAPTER 2

lemon nectar

PJ missed Lemon Pie and the feeling of the little bird's warm body nesting in her curls. Every time she reached up to pat her cropped head she thought about him. But she watched the daily TV news on the rescue operation at the coast and felt proud to think of her bundle of hair mopping oil off the surf. She also eyed the skies, anxious for any sign of Lemon Pie.

And then, yes! During one evening news report she thought she caught a glimpse of a yellow spot, way up on a cliffside. "Look!" she gasped. "Oh . . . was that a flower?"

"Was what a flower?" her mom asked, squinting

at the TV. "What are you talking about, PJ? They're rescuing seabirds and pelicans and you're talking about flowers?"

"Oh, um, way up on the cliff there. Mom, look! Our botany teacher, Mr. Flax, told us how winds carry seeds into cracks in rocks miles and miles away," said PJ. "We have to tell the class when we find flowers or grasses growing out of strange places like rooftops or chimneys or cliffs."

"I don't want you climbing up on the roof to look for flowers," said Mr. Picklelime sternly.

"I won't," PJ promised, and stared at the TV screen. Wait! There it came again. A quick dash of yellow as the helicopter camera zoomed down and hovered over the edge of the cliff.

Lemon Pie! There he sat, in all his glory, on a nest of seagull eggs on a ledge near the top of the cliff, wings spread protectively over his soon-to-be foster chicks. Well, it would be typical of Lemon Pie to float into a nest of lonely eggs if mama seagull was weighed down by oil or had been taken on a rescue boat to be cleaned. All Lemon Pie needed to do was *caw-caw-caw* like a laughing gull and provide loving warmth for the chicks, and how would they know this wasn't their real mama gull?

Lemon Pie was gone in the blink of an eye. The camera zoomed in toward a group of rescuers pulling a raft of oil-covered seabirds out of the surf.

PJ tried to fix the exact location in her memory, picking out landmarks—a huge clump of jagged rocks that made a sort of V in the cliffside down to the beach. If she could find a way to get there, it shouldn't be too difficult to climb down the cliff's edge, should it?

Over the next few days she asked around to see if anyone was planning a trip to the cliffs. But only those involved in the rescue operation could go.

PJ knew it would take weeks for her hair to grow bushy enough to contribute to the mop-up again, but she couldn't wait that long. In her mind, she kept asking Lemon Pie to help her come up with an idea. And then, late that Friday night, she sat bolt upright in bed as the answer came wafting through her window. Warm, gentle winds lifted the fragrance of ripe lemons into her room from Mrs. Patel's trees across the road. *Yes, of course!* She'd create a very special lemonade stand and then find a way to take the lemonade and the money it earned to the rescue crew.

PJ opened her side window and picked out the dark line of lemon trees next to the greenhouse in her favorite neighbor's garden. Mrs. Patel was from Madras, India, and she was so homesick, she had created a wonderfully exotic garden to remind her of her family home. When everything was in full bloom, rows of rich frangipani and lemon blossoms ran all the way to borders of puffy camellias in pink and white. Flaming red bougainvillea cascaded down the whitewashed walls of her house. A magnolia tree, a trellis of jasmine, and a trellis of granadilla gave off delicious scents and cast all sorts of shadows along the pebble path leading to the front door.

Mrs. Patel was a generous neighbor and had told PJ to come over anytime to collect ripe lemons that had fallen into the soft grass.

PJ could hardly wait for morning. There was no way she could fall asleep. So she sat in her window and let the velvety night hug her and gazed up at the Milky Way. She imagined herself running its full length, scattering stardust across the sky with her feet. The feeling was so strong, she reached for her sketch pad and trays of pastels and sketched what was in her mind. But she must have dozed off, head resting on her arms, because she woke as silvery lines were breaking gently into a soft orange horizon.

"*Ommmmm,*" came the familiar sound of Mrs. Patel

meditating in her garden. PJ knew she couldn't interrupt, so she hung out her side window and watched Mrs. Patel doing her morning yoga. PJ loved the tree pose best, when Mrs. Patel balanced on one leg with her hands pressed together in a perfect peak. She stood so still, not even her glossy waist-length hair moved. In her pink yoga pants and loose shirt, she looked like one of those lovely flamingo birds.

As this was Saturday, PJ decided to get dressed in her favorite paint-splashed sweatshirt and jeans. Whenever she wore them, friends told her she matched the floor of an artist's studio. She tiptoed downstairs, left the house, crossed the street, and jumped over the fence onto Mrs. Patel's lawn.

"Oh, hallo, PJ." Mrs. Patel greeted her with a dazzling smile that crinkled her dark eyes. "You're up bright and early today!" she said in her singsong voice.

PJ told Mrs. Patel about her plan for the lemonade stand, and Mrs. Patel ran inside for a basket. Together they picked ripe lemons out of the soft, dewy grass.

"You know, child, lemons can be quite bitter. Come, let's go to my kitchen. Why don't we experiment to see how we can make the sweetest, most unusual lemonade anyone ever tasted?"

For the next hour, they squeezed dozens of lemons into a big glass pitcher and then poured it into ten separate little cups so they could play around with different flavors.

Mrs. Patel reached for her jars of lemon-blossom honey from the bees of their neighbor Mr. Splitzky and stirred in a single teaspoon, then two, then three, to find the right balance between sweet and sour.

"Mmmm," said PJ. "Perfect."

Mrs. Patel wagged her finger. "No, not so fast, PJ. Our search is not yet over. We need a little dash of something else." And with that she opened her cupboard full of pungent spices from Madras. She reached for some bottles, sniffed each one, and shook her head. Finally she picked up a jar of vanilla essence, shook some drops into the lemonade, and held the glass up to the light.

She handed it to PJ and said, "What do you think, child?"

PJ stirred the juice and held it under her nose for a few moments, as Mrs. Patel had done earlier. Then she sipped. And sipped. And sipped. The liquid filled her mouth with a gloriously unusual sweetness and freshness and just a dash of vanilla. It was like nothing she had ever tasted before.

"Come," said Mrs. Patel, clapping her hands. "Let's go into production. We have *dozens* of lemons to squeeze, young lady. No time to waste! Help me make some room in the fridge for the jugs."

Mrs. Patel set up their work space on the counter-top that overlooked her flowering frangipani trees in the garden. She slipped some Indian music into the CD player and showed PJ how to move her fingers in rhythm to turn the lemon squeezing into a special dance of its own.

After PJ and Mrs. Patel made ten jugs, filling the kitchen with the heady scent of lemon, they knew they were almost there. They brought some of the lemon peel outside to dry and stored some in the fridge for Mrs. Patel to use in her homemade chutney. They took left-over pulp to the compost bin at the far end of the garden.

Now it was time to create the lemonade stand. They set up a folding table and stools at the corner of the street where neighbors passed by on foot and bicycles on their way to work or shop. The morning had a warm, creamy softness about it, and since it was Saturday, nobody seemed to be in a frantic rush.

"Let's make it look pretty," Mrs. Patel suggested.

She spread out a yellow handwoven tablecloth with a

bumblebee design. PJ placed two huge pitchers of juice at the front and encircled them with cups. Mrs. Patel put a large round bowl filled to the brim with lemons in the center. But what was missing?

"Hmmm, PJ, go and pick the loveliest frangipani blooms—whole branches—so we can display them in a tall vase, with flowers flowing down to the cloth," she said, handing PJ a pair of scissors.

Before long, Lemon Nectar by Patel and PJ was in business. The first person to stop was old Mr. Kanafani, a Palestinian from the ancient walled city of Jericho who had come to live on the next street with his son and daughter-in-law, both software engineers.

Mr. Kanafani sampled the nectar slowly, eyes closed. Tears rolled down his cheeks. After a few moments, he began to talk about a lemon grove where he used to play as a boy and the soft, ripe lemons with leafy twigs attached he'd pick up off the ground for his mother to slice and place around plates of hummus, beside warm flatbread straight from the oven, bowls of fat local olives, and red radishes. As he spoke, Mr. Kanafani waved the cup of juice around and around in front of his nose, as though moving more and more scenes of his boyhood through his mind.

"*Shukran*," he whispered after a while, "as a Palestinian I lost everything. But not the richness of my memories up here," he added, and tapped his forehead. "Thank you, Mrs. Patel, PJ." He dropped coins into a cup labeled Lemon Pie's Bird Rescue Fund and walked away, tall and thin as a poplar.

Then came the local librarian, Mrs. Martins, from Cape Town, a short, huggable lady with a headful of crisp brown hair and skin the color of chocolate milk. She stopped when she saw the stand, and pressed both hands to her cheeks. Out flooded a torrent of words. "*Ag, nay, nay, nay*, Mrs. Patel, PJ, what are you doing to me? You know I grrrrrew up in District Six in Cape Town and my daddy used to drive around the streets selling lemons off the back of his old *bakkie* truck. And he *always* smelt of lemons, hey? Clothes, shirt, socks, never mind the number of times Mommy scrrrrrubbed and scrrrrrubbed his clothes, hey!

"And *there*," Mrs. Martins pointed at the table, "rrrrright there with the frangipani I loved in Cape Town's gardens and the pile of lemons and everything, you bring my father back to me! Listen, I'm going to cry. I'm going for a little walk and I'll be back in half an hour. Promise you'll keep two cups for me?"

PJ and Mrs. Patel watched her bounce away. They turned and looked at one another. What was happening here?

A group of neighborhood kids suddenly jostled around the table. PJ had to grab the vase of frangipani to prevent it from toppling into the street. The kids poured themselves second cups, asked, "Where are the cookies?" giggled, and pretended to gobble lemon cookies off an invisible plate, spilling juice all over the cloth.

Mrs. Patel clapped her hands sharply. "Off you go, you cheeky children. Go on, off you go, quick!" And off they ran.

Pablo dos Santos y Sanchez pedaled by on his racing bike. He was PJ's dreamily handsome young art teacher with wavy chestnut hair framing his face and almond-shaped eyes. "Aaaaaah!" he said, removing his helmet and gloves and kissing his fingertips to his lips. "The smell of my beloved Andalusia! Ripe lemons and the richest of rich olives and olive oil! Later we will have a feast. I'll bring olives and fresh bread."

And so it went during the day. The word soon spread. By lunchtime, a line snaked around the block. Neighbors began bringing their own chairs and favorite foods to add to the feast. Mr. Splitzky, the "bearded beekeeper," took some of the lemons home and returned with a huge lemon meringue pie.

Mr. Kanafani brought a salad of young lettuce, parsley, and bright red radishes. Mrs. Martins came back with plates of sliced papaya. Ms. Naguri, a Web designer from Japan, walked over from her home four houses away, carrying one of her special rice dishes scattered with sesame seeds. Swiss-born Evi Lenz of the Chocolate Dream arrived with boxes of her special white, milk, and bitter chocolate truffles for everyone to enjoy. She took one sip of the nectar and her eyes widened. Would Mrs. Patel and PJ share their blend with her so she could create a special lemon truffle?

"Of course," said PJ. "As long as you name it Lemon Nectar."

Soon Mrs. Patel's lawn hummed with villagers, all sharing stories with one another over this spontaneous feast.

That evening, Mrs. Patel and PJ counted over two hundred and twenty-six dollars and forty-five cents in coins and small notes. More than that, Pete, the helicopter pilot who took supplies to the coastal relief effort, came by to enjoy the wonderful spread of food. He offered to take Mrs. Patel and PJ on his early-morning flight so they could give the money—and big containers of lemon nectar—to the rescue crew.

PJ was so excited, she wished they could go immediately. Later, after everyone had gone home and she had helped Mrs. Patel clear up, she went to her room and began sketching lemons and frangipani, experimenting with different shades of yellow and cream to get the colors and textures just right.

PJ finally fell asleep and dreamed that the bees on Mrs. Patel's tablecloth came alive and danced with the lemons. She woke up to find drawings and pastels scattered around her pillows.

The next morning she described the exact spot she'd seen on TV, near the long, jagged split in the cliff. Helicopter Pete knew the spot well and said yes, he could certainly land close by so PJ could climb down to see her beloved Lemon Pie. Mrs. Patel and PJ loaded the helicopter with tall containers of lemon nectar and the box of money they had collected for the rescuers.

Pete strapped them into their seats. Propeller rotor blades *whup-whup-whupped* wildly overhead. The chopper lifted high off the ground and arched toward the coast. As they circled close to the cliff's edge, PJ scanned the sky for that quick dash of yellow. But when they drew near, she only saw a laughing gull with a black polka-dot-tipped tail seated in the nest on the ledge just below the top of the cliff, surrounded by chirping chicks.

As promised, Pete swayed down to land a little distance away. PJ asked for time alone. She didn't want to disturb the gull, so she moved very slowly and quietly to the cliff's edge and peeked over. But there was no sign of Lemon Pie anywhere. She looked from left to right, all the way down to the beach below. PJ cupped her hands around her ears to block out all other sounds so she could pick out the quaint call she knew so well. Sadly, there was nothing.

PJ returned to the chopper and hid her face from Pete and Mrs. Patel. Pete tilted to the right, and down they went to a wide stretch of beach that had been turned into a special landing pad. Men and women in shiny oilskins bustled around, unloading supplies.

Whoops and cheers filled the air as they set up the containers and tasted the nectar. They told PJ and Mrs. Patel exactly how Lemon Pie's rescue fund would be used to save more birds.

After returning to the village, Mrs. Patel took PJ's face in her hands and said, "Don't be unhappy, dear PJ. I know about Lemon Pie and how he lived in your hair and the rosebush while you taught him to sing. I'll always keep your secret, please don't worry. But friends like Lemon Pie need to fly and be free, to share the talents you shared with them. Be patient, child. One day you'll look up and hear his song when he is ready to return. Because I know he's in your heart, which is why you wanted the lemons."

When PJ didn't respond, Mrs. Patel added, "See what you did yesterday! We brought lemon joy to the village, to Mr. Kanafani, Mr. Splitzky, Mrs. Martins, Mr. Santos, Ms. Naguri, Ms. Lenz, and who else? We all helped rescue more birds! We've started something, PJ. Come. The village is waiting for more."

PJ knew Mrs. Patel was right, but it just wasn't enough for her to create another lemonade stand in the neighborhood to help save more birds. She yearned to know where Lemon Pie had gone. To keep her little friend's image alive, PJ went up to her room and reached for her sketch pad. Using broad sweeps with her pastels, PJ drew the lost warbler peeking out of clusters of yellow roses that were a little darker than his creamy feathers. She also sketched the TV clip of Lemon Pie swooping close to the cliff's edge and nurturing the nest of laughing gull eggs. Then she sharpened some of her pencils and did quick sketches of everyone who came to the Lemon Nectar fiesta, from poplar-tall Mr. Kanafani to Evi Lenz with her bell-like copper curls, and Mrs. Patel in her flamingo pink yoga pants and shirt.

Smiling, PJ pinned the sketches onto a corkboard, next to the pastels of baskets overflowing with lemons and frangipani blooms she'd drawn the night before. What better way to wake up or fall asleep than facing such delicious sights along with her memories of Lemon Pie?

CHAPTER 3

a birdmail from lemon pie

PJ thought she must be dreaming. There was a frenzied flapping of wings against her windowpane before dawn. She shook herself awake and sat up. But instead of a hundred birds out there, she saw only one, a large white gull with black wings and a handsome polka-dot tail. How could one lone gull kick up such a rumpus?

The gull began to *tap-tap-tap* the windowpane, squawking and yelling "PJ, PJ, PJ, PJ," over and over until PJ thought it would wake up the entire neighborhood. She reached out and opened the window. The gull hopped straight in, clearly annoyed at being kept waiting. He looked a bit battered and travel-weary.

"Are you Ms. PJ Picklelime?" the gull asked.

"Yes I am. And who are you?"

"Special Messenger Gull. I need some form of ID please?"

"Before five o'clock in the morning? You can't be serious!" PJ protested.

"Ms. Picklelime, I take my work *verrrrry* seriously. I have a special delivery for you."

"Delivery?" PJ asked excitedly. "From Lemon Pie?"

The gull nodded twice. "From Lemon Pie. But I have to deliver it to Ms. PJ in person and I was told she had wildly bushy hair. Your hair is too short, so I'll need some ID."

PJ quickly scratched around in the drawer next to her bed for her school ID card and handed it to the gull, who squinted at it, head to one side, one eye shut, and gave the ID back with a brief nod. "All right. But I'm tired and hungry, so before I talk, I need to rest and eat."

"Oh yes, of course." PJ was about to say she knew gulls ate practically anything, when something stopped her. This gull spoke with a different accent than the laughing gulls off the coast, and he seemed bigger and slimmer. Perhaps he had flown a very long way?

"Messenger Gull," she said, "here, I'll make a snug

nest for you in my shoe box." And she went off to her closet and rumpled an old red tartan flannel shirt in the box for the bird. "Now, what would you like to eat?"

The gull hopped gratefully into the box and settled himself around the soft shirt. "Lemon Pie told me you make nice toasted sardine sandwiches. . . ."

"Done," said PJ. "I'll be quiet and quick. My parents are still asleep."

"*Snnnnzzzzz,*" was all she heard from the box.

PJ tiptoed downstairs, trying to figure out Messenger Gull's accent and way of pronouncing *sardines* as "sawdeenes." Mrs. Martins pronounced *sardines* like that. Could Messenger Gull possibly be from somewhere off the coast of South Africa? And he flew all this way? PJ's heart quickened. Had Lemon Pie flown that far? She longed to read Lemon Pie's letter but realized Messenger Gull had probably fallen asleep with it folded under a strong wing.

She prepared the toasted "sawdeene" sandwiches, hoping beyond hope the smell of the toaster wouldn't wake up her parents, and quickly tiptoed back upstairs to her room.

Messenger Gull was lying with one wing fanned out and draped over the edge of the box. PJ placed the sandwich beside the tip of his wing and reached gently under the bird for Lemon Pie's letter. Nothing. The gull stirred, hung out of the box, and began to peck hungrily at the sandwich, murmuring, *"Mmmm, mmmm, mmmm."*

PJ watched for a moment. She went to fill a little bowl with water for him and then asked, "Where do you live, Messenger Gull?"

"Everywhere but nowhere. I fly north to south and east to west delivering birdmail. You have e-mail. We have b-mail. This is how I see the world. I'm a loner, PJ. I'm a Cape gull. I was born on a boat in the docks of Cape Town and learned how to fly off the masts of different boats sailing around the Cape in winds you would never imagine. Never! Winds so fierce and wild they tear feathers off your body and tumble you around the rrrrrugged coastal cliffs. Rocks and proteas fly through the air, and once even a tiny baby baboon went rolling along! I lost my family in a storm. . . . *Mmmm, mmmm,* you know you make the best sandwiches, PJ!"

PJ waited impatiently until Messenger Gull was finished. Then she asked, "When can I get Lemon Pie's letter?"

"Letter?" said Messenger Gull. He leaned over to point his beak into the bowl of water. "Oh no, PJ," the gull chuckled. "You don't understand. There's nothing to read. Once I'm fed and rested, I *quote* Lemon Pie's b-mail to you from memory. Give me a few moments here, hey?" And again PJ heard a little of Mrs. Martins in the way the gull said "hey?"

Finally, Messenger Gull stretched his wings and legs and hopped out of the box. He arranged himself on the window seat like an actor on a stage. "Now, PJ, promise you won't interrupt? Otherwise you'll break my chain of thought."

"I promise!" PJ settled down cross-legged on a big toffee-colored beanbag cushion.

Messenger Gull took some deep breaths and closed his eyes. Outside, a milky white dawn was beginning to break up the dark sky.

"*Lovely PJ,*" Messenger Gull began, in Lemon Pie's crackly little voice.

Tears trickled down PJ's cheeks, and she hastily wiped them away, fearful of interrupting Messenger Gull's flow.

"*Lovely PJ,*" came Lemon Pie's voice again. PJ glanced at the pastels of Lemon Pie pinned up on her corkboard and imagined he was right there in the room with them.

"*Keep watching your windows. I told Messenger Gull to*

remind some of those laughing gulls I took care of to visit you so you wouldn't be lonely," the familiar voice went on. *"I joined some restless gulls who wanted to explore coastlines. We kept going from winter into summer until we found ourselves flying with large Cape gulls down the southeast coast of Africa. To Port Elizabeth. Except one day while flying low over a flooded river bursting to join the sea, I saw these strange little nests looking like baskets swinging in the wind off a tree hanging over the floods. And out flew these little yellow birds, PJ! Imagine! I thought they were South African versions of yellow warblers, but they weren't, because of their funny nests. The birds were called weavers. And I watched one young bird hanging upside down off one of the nests and he was making these silly noises, and you know how silly they must have been, even sillier than I sounded when you first met me. Then he flew away, and a tiny lady bird's head popped out of a hole in the side of the nest and said, 'Hey, you!'"* (Messenger Gull created a falsetto voice in a South African accent for Lady Weaver.)

" *'Me?' I said, looking around."* (Lemon Pie's voice.)

" *'Yes you. Come here.'"* (Lady Weaver's voice.)

" *'Come there?' I asked."* (Lemon Pie's voice.)

" *'What's the matter with you?'"* (Lady Weaver's voice.)

"Well, you know me, PJ. Without another peep I flew over. And I looked up into this cute little face and felt all fluttery

until Lady Weaver said, 'Don't get funny ideas, stranger. I don't need to know who you are. But I need you to hang around so they will stop bothering me!'

" 'They?'

" 'You don't want to know. Hop in.' And she disappeared.

"So there I was, PJ, invited to become Lemon Pie, Chief Bouncer. I puffed out my chest and climbed on board Lady Weaver's nest. She taught me how to dangle upside down off the nest, hanging on by my claws and swaying in the wind. All those noisy birds bothering her laughed and asked who her 'freaky friend' was. But I'm so used to being different, it didn't bother me. All I could think was how boring they were. Lady Weaver and I became buddies. It made me think of you, PJ, because I haven't had a good buddy since leaving you."

Messenger Gull sipped some water and then continued.

"Lady Weaver told me about the floods that tore walls off houses and swept beaches into the sea and toppled tall palm trees that floated by like matchsticks. But even that force couldn't destroy the weavers' nests. Even though they swung and bucked dizzily in the storm, not one of them broke. Out came the TV crews and cameras, and they were on the evening news. But Lady Weaver told me she could do without the fame, because all those scruffy birds kept harassing her, thinking they could just move in and freeload. *'I'm very fussy about boyfriends,' she said."*

Messenger Gull paused. The room became very quiet. He looked up at the corkboard. "Your Lemon Pie looks a little scruffier than that now, PJ. Listen, do you have any bananas downstairs?" he asked.

"Oh, oh yes, of course," she said. She scrambled up and paused by the door to make sure her parents were still asleep. She returned in minutes with a plate of bananas and a knife and began peeling and slicing the fruit to share with Messenger Gull. He hopped down off the window seat and snuggled beside her.

"*Mmmm*, nice, but not as dark and sweet as South African bananas."

"These are from Guatemala. Don't be rude!" PJ said.

Messenger Gull chuckled. He pecked at the banana bits, slurped some more water, and hopped back on the window seat. "Now, where was I?"

"Lady Weaver told Lemon Pie she was fussy about boyfriends."

"Oh yes, yes, yes, now let me pick up the thread here . . . hmmmmm . . . yes. . . . *Well, once the rascals . . .*" Messenger Gull cleared his throat, closed his eyes, and went on talking in Lemon Pie's voice. "*Once those rascals stopped harassing Lady Weaver, she had no more use for me, you see, PJ. She fed me one morning and said I had to move on. That was it. So I flew toward the Indian Ocean, hoping to meet some of the Cape gulls, as I felt a little lost. I'd been too comfortable for a while. And then, PJ, as I flew past the port with the big rusty storage tanks, you will never guess what happened."*

"What?" asked PJ.

"Shhh," warned Messenger Gull. "Don't interrupt me!"

"Oh, sorry."

Messenger Gull paused, frowning, then, once again in Lemon Pie's voice, he said, *"You'll never guess what happened. I saw this huge tree by the port. So huge and bushy it reminded me of your hair, PJ, so I flew straight into it and perched on a branch. The sparkling blue Indian Ocean was behind me. And I faced a busy crossroads, opposite a steep hill with a bright green mosque and roads going from left to right. The tree was next to the port, in a scrubby field with piles of builders' rubble, bricks, and broken bottles. The tree was full of birds. Some sounded like Canada geese but didn't look like them. Oh, guinea fowl and peahens and colorful little birds I had never seen before, with bright turquoise tails. So, I began to twitter away in the voice you trained and didn't feel shy or embarrassed about not sounding like a true yellow warbler, because I was the only warbler around! There were also a few Cape gulls—wow, are they noisy—and some of those rascal weavers I chased away from Lady Weaver's nest, who found it very funny to hear she had finally chased me away, too!*

"We all got talking and they told me about the area around the port, called South End, where many wonderful families of all different colors and backgrounds and religions used to live. Many of them worked at the docks or on the fishing boats and factories close by. Only, the government was very cruel in those days and said only white families could live there. So the police came in with big bulldozers and smashed all the houses and shops—that's why the field by the tree was bare except for piles of broken bricks and glass. And they sent Chinese families to the Chinese areas. Black families to the black areas. Mixed-race families to the mixed-race areas. Muslim families to the Muslim areas. Indian families to the Indian areas. They broke up the whole neighborhood, PJ. Isn't that sad? But you know what happened? The white families refused to remain behind once the area was destroyed and all their friends were sent away. So they moved away, too."

Messenger Gull shook his head and paused to sip some water.

PJ looked down, feeling the sadness he shared. Then she lifted her head and listened. The house was beginning to stir.

"I'm almost done," said Messenger Gull before resuming Lemon Pie's voice.

"I forgot to tell you what kind of tree this was. It's a huge wild fig tree, PJ, and I mean huge, like a million times bigger than your hair, with a gnarled, twisted trunk. When South End was destroyed all those years ago, it stopped producing figs. Just stopped like that. But you know what? As I sit here, I can see tiny figs beginning to bud again, because there's a democratic government now. All sorts of people can live, work, and study where they want. I'll stay here and wait with the other birds until the fruit is ripe. Then I will eat a lot of it and fly away to drop and plant its seeds all along the coast to Cape Town. So goodbye, dear PJ. I love you!"

PJ bit her lip. Messenger Gull began to cry big drops of salty tears.

"And that's it?" asked PJ. "Lemon Pie said he was just going to keep on flying?"

Messenger Gull nodded. He wiped away his tears with the tip of a wing and stared outside at the pink sky.

PJ sighed. After a quiet moment, she thanked Messenger Gull for the wonderful b-mail from Lemon Pie.

"Will you stay with me, Messenger Gull, so I can send a b-mail back to Lemon Pie?"

Messenger Gull shook his head sadly. "I wouldn't know where to find your Lemon Pie," he said. "Now I have to fly to Central Park in New York to deliver a b-mail to a silver-gray dove who lives in a tree by the boat basin."

And with that, he pecked up the last of the banana pieces, hopped on the windowsill, spread his wings, and lifted off into the sky.

Mr. Flax, the botany teacher, was setting up his Power-Point as PJ rushed in late. Pencils tumbled out of her backpack and clattered all over the floor. Mr. Flax was a gangly, craggy man with smiling blue eyes, and he said to the class, "Seeds scatter just like our PJ's pencils. Look!" He began showing various views of his garden that he had photographed last summer. Tall, wavy sunflowers zigzagged across a path and made crazy patterns on the lawn and soared out of beds of lavender and mint.

"Oooh." "Oh wow." "Cool." "Look at that!" everyone said at once.

"I didn't plant any of those sunflowers," Mr. Flax chuckled. "Nature did the work. They're all spontaneous. In some areas they sprouted out of compost. Or they grew out of seeds dropped by birds around the bird feeder. Or breezes brought them onto my path from sunflower farms in the next village. Come and look at what I saved," he said, scattering sunflower seeds on his desk along with dried sunflowers, brittle stalks, and roots from his shed.

PJ remembered an earlier class when he had prompted them to be aware of tiny plants and trees sprouting out of crags and crevices in the cliffside. She felt thrilled, thinking about Lemon Pie's plan to scatter seeds from the big fig tree by the port all the way down South Africa's south coast.

"Mr. Flax," she asked, "do sunflowers also grow out of trees when they fall down and rot and go all crumbly?"

"Good question, PJ. What do the rest of you think?"

Hands shot up. "Sunflowers need sun, don't they?" piped a voice from the back.

"Sure." Mr. Flax nodded. "I've seen sunflowers growing out of rotting tree trunks. Their stalks bend every which way to tilt their faces to the sun."

"Broken trees in our backyard are full of creepy-

crawlies and funny mushroomy plants. But no
ers," said another voice from the front of the class.

"Creepy-crawlies, heat, and rain help to break down
the inside of a tree into all sorts of ecosystems," said Mr.
Flax. "In some places deep in the rain forests, you'll find
beautiful orchids, ferns, or mosses growing out of old
tree trunks lying on the ground." Turning to the white-
board, he reached for green, red, and brown markers and
began writing out their homework assignment for the
next class. "See how many forms of life you can find in
any old broken tree trunk. Spiders weaving webs. Mush-
rooms. All kinds of grasses. Twisted roots. Wildflowers,
or maybe some young sunflowers?"

"Bugs?" PJ suggested.

"As many as you can spot," said Mr. Flax. "Only don't
touch anything in case hundreds of fire ants come scurry-
ing out!"

waterfalls

"Jump in, PJ," said Mrs. Patel, rattling to a stop outside PJ's school in an old VW Beetle of a brilliant rose red like the bougainvillea tumbling over her house.

"Oh, Mrs. Patel, I have homework," pleaded PJ.

"No arguments," said Mrs. Patel. She wagged her finger so fast, her jangly bracelets sounded like castanets. "I'll have you home before sunset. Here, let me call your mom," she added. She reached for her cell phone and speed-dialed the Picklelime home to leave a message.

"Done," she said. "Come. I want to show you my waterfall." And with that, she spun the VW around in a single motion and sped off toward the cliffs.

PJ eyed the sky just in case young Lemon Pie had decided to fly home, but in her heart she knew that was impossible. She told Mrs. Patel about the wonderful surprise in Messenger Gull's b-mail and how Lemon Pie had ended up in the huge old wild fig tree down by the harbor of Port Elizabeth on the east coast of South Africa.

"A wild fig tree? Did he say anything special about it?" asked Mrs. Patel.

"Special? Well, it was filled with all sorts of birds, waiting to eat new figs."

"No, there's more. Didn't Lemon Pie tell you the wild fig tree is sacred in southern Africa?"

"Sacred?" PJ said in surprise.

"You see, PJ," Mrs. Patel went on, pausing at a red light. "For hundreds of years, families have gone to wild fig trees to talk to their ancestors and to ask for messages and guidance."

"Their ancestors also lived in the wild fig tree?" PJ asked, puzzled.

Mrs. Patel laughed. The light turned green and the VW *varoomed* ahead. "No, child. The ancestors had passed on, one by one, invisible to us but all there in the memories of their loved ones. When family members had a problem and needed to sort something out, they would visit the wild fig tree."

"I don't think Lemon Pie knew that, but he wants to drop wild fig seeds along the coast. Isn't that great? More trees for more families to visit!"

"What a lovely idea!" said Mrs. Patel, moving the VW's stick shift down to a lower gear.

Fascinated, PJ watched her. She was used to her mom's Toyota automatic. They slowed down, turned onto a dirt track, and bounced over potholes toward the craggy clifftops.

"Mrs. Patel, how do you know about the wild fig tree?" she asked.

"Ah, that's simple, PJ. You see, many Indian families went to live and work in South Africa's sugar plantations a long time ago, mainly around a city called Durban on the east coast. It's very hot and tropical and steamy and lush. Pineapples and bananas are deep gold in color and they are so sweet they make your head spin! I have uncles and aunties there and more cousins than I can count. That's how I know about the wild fig tree. Your Lemon Pie will come back to us as a wise little bird after all these experiences."

PJ was silent for a moment, trying to recall everything

Messenger Gull told her about Lemon Pie's travels. She hung out the window to study the slope of the cliffs. Jagged ledges held wisps of former nests where Lemon Pie once protected the eggs of local laughing gulls. When would she meet some of those gulls, as Lemon Pie promised?

The beach seemed equally stark after the oil spill and massive cleanup operation. Only a couple of dark shapes dotted the sand here and there where a stray oil streak had escaped the cleanup and floated back with the tides. PJ touched her tight, springy curls. When they grew wildly bushy again, perhaps the coast guard would ask for more sacks of hair.

The VW pulled up close to a pathway cut into the cliff. Mrs. Patel switched off the noisy motor and said, "Listen, PJ!"

PJ opened the car door and raised her head. She could hear the distant *caw-caw* of gulls and steady lapping of the ocean below.

"Listen beyond those sounds," said Mrs. Patel. "Come, let me show you."

They got out of the VW. Mrs. Patel dropped to her knees and lowered her ear to the sand between clumps of sea oats. When PJ hunkered down and did the same, a deafening roar filled her head. She sat up quickly and looked around, thinking she'd heard the *whup-whup* of Pete's helicopter.

"Oh no, child." Mrs. Patel stood up. "This is a surprise. . . . I want you to see for yourself."

"See what, Mrs. Patel?"

"Follow the sounds, PJ."

They climbed down the stone pathway, holding on to the rope hung there as a handrail. Then PJ began to tune her ears in to the roar of water.

Halfway down the cliff, Mrs. Patel said, "Turn around, PJ. Look!"

There it was. A waterfall crashed down inside the ravine and hit a pool that jumped from the impact. Water escaped over the edge in three separate waterfalls that plunged wildly into another pool below, so deep it looked almost purple to PJ. She leaned over.

Mrs. Patel grabbed hold of her T-shirt. "Careful, PJ! You're too young for the waterfalls to take you. Let's keep going, to my secret hiding place."

They climbed all the way down to the lower pool. Water swirled and whirled and splashed over the rocks. PJ followed Mrs. Patel along the path to a sandy ledge and into a cave directly behind the rushing curtains of

clear water. A wild roar filled the air. "Oooh *wow*," PJ said. Mrs. Patel waved her closer. A thousand stings of spray hit them. Sand squelched underfoot. They were soaked within seconds.

They stood there until their ears rang with the noise. Then they returned to the path and followed the rapid streams that fanned out across the beach toward the waves. Clear, sweet waters met salt in a joyful leap of foam.

Close by, PJ found a large, seaweed-covered tree that had floated in with the tide. Tiny crabs scurried around and vanished into crevices in the roots as she crouched down for a closer look. Mussels and shells crusted an entire side. Mr. Flax hadn't said anything about trees that washed up on the beach, but wasn't this a perfect example of a different ecosystem for the class? She took a quick mental snapshot of it to sketch later for her homework.

The sun hovered over the horizon like a big, squashy overripe orange. Softer shades of orange lingered across the sky between cloud puffs. PJ closed her eyes because she didn't want to watch the sun disappear. But the air was becoming chillier, giving both PJ and Mrs. Patel goose bumps.

They retraced their steps and climbed up the path,

stopping once more to watch the waters crashing down relentlessly in the falling light.

Mrs. Patel reached into the backseat of the VW for huge, fluffy midnight blue towels and handed one to PJ. They dried themselves and their damp hair and sipped cups of spicy hot chai she had brought in a thermos.

Mrs. Patel said, "Come, child. Time we were on our way." Then, turning, she pointed toward the mountain. "Oh, PJ, look at the moon!"

PJ took a deep breath. As the squashy orange sun sank into the ocean, directly opposite it, the curve of the moon began to rise between two peaks. "I've never seen both at the same time before! This is *awesome*, Mrs. Patel. *Awesome!* Please can't we stay a little longer? *Please?*"

Mrs. Patel glanced at her watch and shook her head. "PJ, I promised your mother I'd get you home by sunset!"

"Aw, just a few more minutes. Can't we call her?"

Mrs. Patel jangled her car keys. "Let's go, PJ. Keep the beautiful images in your thoughts. Never wait until they're all over."

"I don't want to go home," PJ announced.

"What nonsense! Come. It's warmer in the car. Talk to me, child," she said, switching on the ignition. The

VW jumped to life and they bounced over the potholes once again, toward the road.

"I don't know what to say," PJ mumbled after a moment.

"You're too young to be so sad."

"Only older people can feel sad?" PJ asked.

Mrs. Patel chuckled. "Lemon Pie has gone, but there are other birds and animals that need you. No time to waste now." Pursing her lips and making a swift left turn, she said, "I think I know just the thing for you! A big sister. Have you met Ruth?"

"Ruth? The girl who bikes around with her hands off the handlebars? Joshua's her twin?"

"That's Ruth."

"But she has all kinds of friends. She probably thinks I'm a baby," PJ said.

"Nonsense! I'll introduce you. She lives a few streets away from us. Do you know what she does?"

"I think she plays soccer?"

"Oh, much more than that, child! She rescues injured animals. She could probably do with some help. She's hoping a soccer scholarship will pay for veterinary school in a few years. So she's getting lots of experience right now."

Mrs. Patel pulled up outside PJ's front gate. "Off you go now, PJ. Your mother's probably wondering what's happened to you. I'll take you to meet Ruth after school tomorrow."

"Thanks, Mrs. Patel. Also, thanks for sharing your waterfalls with me," said PJ, climbing out of the VW. "The sun and moon put on a great show for us, don't you think?"

"Oh yes, PJ. Just keep watching the sky." Mrs. Patel laughed.

※

Later, at the kitchen table, PJ told her parents about the wonderful sights she had seen.

Her dad took another slice of spinach quiche and said, "Shouldn't you be doing homework instead of chasing waterfalls? Patel's claptrap VW is so noisy I'm surprised the waterfalls didn't dry up in shock!"

"Philip, don't be such a party pooper," Mrs. Picklelime said, helping herself to fresh beetroot-and-parsley salad. Then, with a toss of the head, she said to PJ, " 'Dance there upon the shore; What need have you to care For wind or water's roar? And tumble out your hair That the *salt drops have wet; Being young you have not known The fool's triumph . . .' "*

"Maura, give us a break," PJ's dad cut in. "PJ's too young for your mad Irish poets."

"No one's ever too young for Yeats," PJ's mom said. "My parents read him to me in my crib."

"Well, that explains a lot," he muttered.

"Dad, Mom, come on," pleaded PJ. Then she turned to Mrs. Picklelime. "Mom, what's the poem called? Won't you finish it for me? I like the words."

"Ah, it's called 'To a Child Dancing in the Wind,' and yes, of course I can finish it for you. Where was I now?"

" 'The fool's triumph,' Maura, 'the fool's triumph,' " said Mr. Picklelime, rising from his chair. "OK, I'll leave you poets to it. I'm beat." He went to the next room to watch TV.

"Mom?"

Mrs. Picklelime glanced at her husband's half-finished meal, then reached out and closed the door to muffle the sound of the TV. In a soft tone, she went on, " '. . . *nor yet Love lost as soon as won* . . .' " Her voice trailed off. "Um, sorry, PJ, I can't remember the rest. Have a look at my collected poems of W. B. Yeats. It's on one of the bookshelves in the front room," she said.

PJ tried to figure out her mother's expression, but Mrs. Picklelime looked away. "Mom, did you quote poetry to me as a baby?"

"Sure I did, honey. It's a long tradition in my family. My ear is never far from wonderful poets and writers— Yeats, Lorca, Keats, Rumi, Frost, Angelou. You'll find them all there, all of them," she added, nodding in the direction of the bookshelves. "Love them in your time, PJ. Now, let's stack the dishwasher!"

Later PJ went up to her room. Why did her parents seem to be in different worlds these days? To stop herself from worrying, she completed her homework assignments, including a detailed pencil sketch of the mussel- and seaweed-covered tree she found on the sand. Then she picked up her pastels, propped herself comfortably against cushions on her window seat, and began to draw Messenger Gull flapping at her window. Before going to sleep, she also sketched the waterfalls, the beach, the squashy orange sunset on the horizon, and the moon peeping above the mountains.

CHAPTER 5

ruth and the rescue animals

The next afternoon after school, ready to work with Ruth's animals, PJ changed into blue-and-white-striped dungarees and a dark blue shirt. Mrs. Patel met her at the front gate and they walked together to Ruth's place a few blocks away.

Everyone in the neighborhood knew Ruth's garden. Massive live oak trees grew every which way. PJ nicknamed them the "arms-and-legs" trees. Huge trunks splayed out of deep roots surrounding the house, back and front. Branches sprawled wide and high at the top and also curved and snaked close to the ground, like some mythical sea creature that couldn't stop growing. The two-story house was built sort of zigzag around the trees. Vine-covered branches poked in and out of balconies.

Ruth's tree house nestled in the curve of a giant trunk and balanced on two thick branches. When Ruth saw PJ and Mrs. Patel, she hung over the top half of her Dutch door and grinned at them. She wore a large, bright purple T-shirt. Her honey-colored hair was loosely braided into a wide pigtail that dangled in midair.

Mrs. Patel said, "Ruth, here's PJ. She has a wonderful way with birds and I thought you could do with an extra pair of hands."

"*Cool!*" Ruth said, waving at PJ. She opened the lower half of the door and tossed a rope ladder down from the tree house. Rolling her eyes, she explained, "I keep the ladder up here because my twin Joshua's going crazy with a tiny camcorder zooming in on anything that moves. The animals freak! Come on up, PJ."

"Girls, I'll leave you to it," said Mrs. Patel. She hugged PJ goodbye.

PJ swung herself up the rope ladder and grabbed Ruth's hand at the top to jump inside. Her first glimpse made her gasp. Ruth's tree house was something every kid dreamed of having. The walls, floor, and ceiling were crafted out of raw planks of oak salvaged from trimmed branches. The tree house was tall enough for an adult and roomy enough for PJ to stretch out her arms and make two complete circles in each direction. Later she found out it had been built by their neighbor Mr. "Bearded Beekeeper" Splitzky as a mini version of his barn.

"I love it! Great woody smell. Does Joshua have his own tree house?" PJ asked.

Ruth shook her head. "His bedroom's twice the size of mine and full of junk. I chose the tiny bedroom, so my parents had the tree house built for me."

Books filled corner shelves. One shelf held a soccer ball and a team photograph. Big, puffy bright blue cushions lay below a sloping skylight. Four homemade cages painted in vivid reds and greens stood stacked two by two in the opposite corner under screened windows. Ruth opened the first cage and gently removed an injured red cardinal.

"This is Cardy," she explained. "I found him tangled in a fence one afternoon. He was scared and tore some of his wing feathers. He wasn't *badly* injured, but he couldn't take care of himself. So I cleaned him up and treated his cuts. Maybe tomorrow we'll see if he'll fly."

"Can I hold him?"

"Mmmm, better not, he's still a little nervous," Ruth said, smoothing his brilliant red feathers. The bird nestled into Ruth's hand as though he had been born there. PJ began to tell Ruth about Lemon Pie.

Ruth nodded. "I hear you, PJ. It's tough when you get attached. But birds need to fly around feeling the winds for thousands of miles. You're lucky your friend sent a b-mail."

Ruth seemed very wise for a thirteen-year-old. Her intense gray eyes were flecked with gold. PJ wondered if animals looked into them and felt a special connection. She watched Ruth place Cardy in his little cage, shake some birdseed into his dish, and lock the cage carefully.

"Do you like jazz flute?" Ruth asked. "We love it." She leaned over to select something from her laptop and turned up the speakers. All sorts of birdlike chirps and twirly sounds filled the tree house. Ruth and Cardy began bobbing their heads at one another in time to the music.

PJ smiled and told Ruth how she used melodious sounds to help Lemon Pie develop his voice.

"Great. Maybe you can do the same for Oohoo?" Ruth said as she reached into the next cage. A fat owl sat in there, huge eyes staring out of a motley of fluffy gray, brown, and rust-colored feathers. If PJ didn't know she was a live owl, she'd have thought Oohoo was one of those owl dolls people used on their roofs to scare seagulls away. The flute music hit a high note in the background. Unlike Cardy, the owl showed no response.

"I can't figure Oohoo out," confessed Ruth, eye to eye with the owl. Holding Oohoo aloft, she lowered herself cross-legged onto one of the blue cushions. PJ sank down into the other cushion, opposite her.

"I thought Oohoo was blind," Ruth explained. "I found her sitting under a tree one morning looking exactly as she is looking at you now. You don't normally see owls by day. They're night creatures. When I realized she wasn't blind, I decided she was catatonic."

Puzzled, PJ looked at the owl and back at Ruth. "She thinks she's a cat?"

Ruth giggled and ruffled the owl's feathers with her nose. "If only! 'Catatonic' means Oohoo's freaked into a sort of frozen state. Maybe a hawk chowed down on her babies or something."

"Oh wow. Poor Oohoo," PJ said.

"You can hold her, PJ. Here, she likes her little ears to be rubbed. Be gentle but firm. She won't peck you. See, she's puffing out her chest. Isn't she *cute*?" Ruth said *cute* in a squeaky little voice. "See how soft her feathers are?"

PJ cupped her hands and reached out for the owl. Oohoo was much bigger than Lemon Pie, but she felt the owl's warmth and was sure Oohoo leaned into her hands. Yes, Oohoo even dropped her head so PJ could scratch behind her ears.

"Hey, PJ, she *likes* you." Ruth smiled and lowered the volume on the speakers. "She doesn't usually respond like that. Go, *girl*!"

"If you haven't heard her hoot, why do you call her Oohoo?" PJ asked.

"It's Swiss German for 'owl.' You know the Chocolate Dream? Ms. Lenz is from Basel. She noticed me rescuing Oohoo and named her on the spot."

PJ loved Ms. Lenz's store. Wonderful bronze fountains of molten white and milk chocolate stood in the Dream's front window. Deliciously sweet smells wafted out to the street from morning to night. When was Ms. Lenz going to create the special Lemon Nectar chocolate they had talked about during the lemonade-stand party? An idea jumped into her mind.

PJ looked into Oohoo's eyes and said, "I don't believe you're catawhatzit. You and I are going to work together. Starting tomorrow. We may need to pay Ms. Lenz a little visit, of course, so she can see how you're doing."

"Go for it, PJ. Any excuse for chocolate, right?" Ruth laughed.

Oohoo kept staring at PJ as Ruth took the owl, opened the cage door, and placed Oohoo back on her perch. PJ liked the confident way Ruth handled the owl. She made it look so easy.

"Now it's Squirt's turn," said Ruth, reaching into the third cage. Squirt the squirrel came soaring out and jumped all over the tree house. He was a combo of spiky gray fur with the softest golden belly, which he enjoyed showing off. He sort of matched Ruth's eyes, PJ thought. Squirt spiraled from the cushions to the bookshelves, sent the soccer ball bouncing to the floor, and flew at full stretch onto Ruth's shoulder. He made annoyed *brrrk-brrrkbrrrk* sounds and flicked her honey-blond pigtail with his bushy tail.

Ruth flicked his tail in response. "Squirt's just about ready to leave," she said. "He was attacked by something and I found him dragging his leg across the lawn. Look at how he moves now!" She shook nuts into a dish and tried to lower him from her shoulder. But Squirt dug his back claws into her shirt and dangled down like a large exclamation mark, nose twitching around the bowl.

"Oh, Squirt, you're a piece of work," said Ruth.

"Tomorrow we'll open the windows and let you jump around out there." She nodded at the huge branches swaying outside the tree house.

"Do they come back and visit once they leave you?" PJ asked.

"Sometimes. I know Squirt will," said Ruth, ruffling the fur down the full length of his spine while he continued to crunch nuts. "Cardy's family lives in the bushes a few houses away, so he won't go too far. As for Oohoo, who knows?" Ruth tugged her pigtail and gazed at the owl's cage for a few minutes. "Do you think she needs one of those bird shrinks, PJ?"

"No." PJ shook her head. "She needs me."

"Hey, RUTH!" A voice yelled from below.

"I'm BUSY!" Ruth yelled back.

"RUTH!" The voice was loud and impatient.

Placing a protective hand over Squirt, Ruth rose and looked over the Dutch door. "Joshua, are you deaf?" she called down. "I'm *busy*. PJ, come and say hi to my other half."

Both girls hung over the door. Joshua stood below, legs apart, hands on hips. His thick, bouncy honey-blond hair was the same color as Ruth's but splashed over his shoulders and practically covered his face. He wore black-rimmed glasses, a black T-shirt, black jeans, and red-and-white-striped high-tops. His eyes matched Ruth's.

"Hey, PJ." He waved. "Are you staying for dinner? Mom's making enough pasta to feed the world." Joshua's voice was all crackly, just about to break.

"Wow, some other time maybe, you guys. I need to go. My mom's probably out looking for me," she said.

Ruth tossed the rope ladder to the ground. "See you after school tomorrow? Joshua, hold the ladder steady for PJ. Can't you see it's wobbling?"

"Bye, Ruth. Thanks for a great time," said PJ as she climbed down.

"You're welcome," Joshua said. He held the ladder with one hand and grinned up at his twin. "Coming, too, Ruth? Or do we call room service?"

When PJ returned home, she found her mom eating alone at the kitchen table, reading a book.

"Where's Dad?"

"He went out for a walk," said Mrs. Picklelime. She got up to ladle bean-and-veggie soup for PJ out of a large glass pot bubbling happily on the stove.

"Thanks, Mom, this smells *so* good," said PJ, taking her bowl to the table. They sat there enjoying soup and crusty whole-wheat bread while PJ told her mother about Ruth's tree house and Squirt, Oohoo, and Cardy and the funny way the twins spoke to one another.

"It's a wonderful opportunity for you, PJ," Mrs. Picklelime said. Then she launched into, " *'The Owl and the Pussy-Cat went to sea in a beeeeee-you-tiful pea-green boat: They took some honey, and plenty of money . . .'* "

"Mom, be serious," giggled PJ.

"Who wants to be serious? It's *sooooo* boring," said Mrs. Picklelime.

Later PJ sketched the tree house in the wavy oak tree, with Ruth in her purple T-shirt, Oohoo, Cardy, and Squirt, while her mom read all sorts of poetry to her about wild swans and goats that she didn't really understand. Long after she went to bed, PJ finally heard her dad unlock the front door.

CHAPTER 6

the chocolate dream

After school the next day, PJ collected Oohoo from Ruth's tree house and hid the owl down the front of her mottled gray-and-brown peasant shirt. PJ had picked the shirt that would best blend with the owl's feathers. She started on her bike toward the Chocolate Dream but decided to swing around to see Mrs. Patel first.

"PJ, slow down, child," said Mrs. Patel. "The way you cycled around that corner! Are Mr. Splitzky's bees chasing you? And what's that in your shirt?" Mrs. Patel lowered her shears and smoothed clippings off the top of her flowering purple sage hedge into a bucket for her compost pile.

PJ parked her bike against the sidewalk and opened the top buttons of her shirt. The tips of Oohoo's ears popped up.

"Good grief, PJ! First you're hiding birds in your hair. Now they're down your shirt. Whatever is next? Who's this?"

"Oohoo the owl, Mrs. Patel. Ruth says she's catatonic, so I'm taking things slowly. What makes a bird catatonic?"

Mrs. Patel stared at the bulge in PJ's shirt. "Trauma, PJ. Your new friend has seen something *dreadful.* Otherwise she wouldn't just sit there like a statue. But"—Mrs. Patel nodded—"it's good for her to feel your heartbeat."

"I also like to feel hers." PJ laughed. "I'm rehabbing her."

"How, child?" Mrs. Patel continued to snip stray branches off her hedge.

PJ rubbed some of the cut sprays of purple sage between her hands so she could enjoy their lovely smell. At that moment, their neighbor "bearded beekeeper" Mr. Splitzky ambled by with his caramel-colored retriever mix, Blossom. Ever curious, Blossom lifted her head and sniffed, nose twitching.

Knowing the dog sensed more in the air than humans and purple sage, PJ placed a protective hand over Oohoo.

"Afternoon, Mrs. Patel. Afternoon, PJ," Mr. Splitzky said.

"Afternoon, Mr. Splitzky," they chorused.

"C'mon, Bloss," he said. He gave the retriever's leash a tug. Blossom followed him but kept glancing back at PJ.

"She's wondering why I don't ruffle and cuddle her," PJ said. When they were out of earshot, she added, "I didn't want to get too close in case she scared Oohoo." PJ stroked the front of her shirt until she could feel the owl relax and soften against her.

"Do you sing to Oohoo, PJ?" Mrs. Patel asked. She put down her shears and reached for the bucket.

"No. She doesn't react to humming. I just do the deep breathing you taught me."

"Keep doing that, PJ, when she's close to you like this. Remember, if you get agitated, she could try to claw her way out of your shirt. So be careful."

PJ smiled. "Thanks, Mrs. Patel, I'll remember. Bye!" She remounted her bike and headed over to the chocolate shop. Blindfolded, she could easily have found her way through the streets to Ms. Lenz, not just because she loved the route, but because wafts of chocolate got stronger and stronger as she approached, especially when the air was warm.

Ms. Evi Lenz was in the Dream's window, adjusting the chocolate fountains. She wore a green apron patterned with dancing goats and milk buckets. She also wore a matching green bandanna around her forehead to keep her cluster of bell-like copper curls from bouncing around her face. Every time she nodded or laughed, PJ heard a tinkling sound from the curls. She waved cheerfully as PJ parked her bike outside and met her at the door.

"Hi, Ms. Lenz."

"*Grüezi*, PJ," she replied. Ms. Lenz always used a friendly Swiss German greeting when she saw PJ. She dropped her eyes and stared at the owl's ears brushing PJ's throat and said, "I don't believe this. You brought Oohoo to see me?"

PJ undid a few more buttons. Ms. Lenz placed both hands on her knees and leaned over to stare into Oohoo's eyes. "Wise Oohoo," she said, "I miss hearing you at night. Come to think of it, I don't hear any owls at night." Ms. Lenz rose, turned to PJ, and frowned. "PJ, why are the owls so quiet?"

PJ was equally puzzled. "I hadn't noticed. But I'll stay up late and listen tonight!" she offered.

Oohoo blinked and then closed her eyes.

Evi Lenz said, "Hmmm, *she* knows why. She will let

you know in her special way." Ms. Lenz turned toward a glass-front display cabinet and opened it up at the back. The top shelves were lined with her handmade assorted truffles in dark, milk, and white chocolate. Pralines and the boxed varieties were below. Framed pictures of all her truffle and praline varieties hung on the wall behind her.

"Oohoo, look what you're missing!" said PJ, patting the front of her shirt.

"Oh, wait for the best!" said Ms. Lenz. She reached into the cabinet and removed a small tray of white chocolate truffles lightly sprinkled with tiny slivers of lemon peel.

"*Alllllso,*" she said proudly, "Lemon Nectar . . . inspired by Mrs. Shanti Patel and PJ Picklelime! Go on, help yourself. Tell me what you think."

PJ hesitated. "Shouldn't Mrs. Patel be here to try it with me?"

Evi Lenz smiled. "She will come later. Don't worry, PJ. Best you try them separately so you don't influence one another. Trust me. I know!"

PJ reached out and popped a round lemon truffle into her mouth.

"Let it melt slowly," Ms. Lenz advised. "Don't chew."

PJ kept the round truffle between her tongue and palate and resisted the temptation to roll it around in her mouth like a fireball. It began to dissolve. Her eyelids fluttered. The intense lemon-flavored center was richer than the Lemon Nectar drink she had concocted with Mrs. Patel that day! She tried to talk, but it came out as a gurgle. She waited a few more minutes, then said, "No way will I brush my teeth tonight. I want to taste lemon when I wake up tomorrow morning!"

"Now, PJ, don't go that far!" Ms. Lenz scooped a few of the truffles into a little box patterned with dancing lemons. She closed it with a pretty yellow ribbon and the Dream label. "For you and your parents to enjoy as dessert!" she said.

"Ms. Lenz?"

"Yes, *spätzli*?" she said. PJ loved it when she called her "little sparrow" in Swiss German.

"Can I take some for Ruth and Joshua?" PJ asked.

Ms. Lenz wagged her finger and said, "Just two each for those twins. Otherwise they'll gobble them up like M&M's and taste nothing! Teach them how to enjoy your special truffles *slowly*, PJ," she added, placing four Lemon Nectars in another little box with a matching yellow ribbon. She put both boxes in a bag. "Now remember, I'm depending on you, your parents, Mrs. Patel, and the twins to give me feedback."

"They taste *perfect*!"

"For you, yes, but let's hear from the others. PJ, you're my test market. I want to know if the truffles are too sweet, not sweet enough, too lemony, not lemony enough, too creamy, or not creamy enough. Try another one a bit later. Then tell me what your parents and friends have to say."

As if on cue, Oohoo began to move around in the front of PJ's shirt.

"No, Oohoo," said Ms. Lenz, tapping the owl through PJ's shirt. "Owls and chocolate don't mix. Unless they're Swiss owls!"

PJ giggled and said, "Thanks, Ms. Lenz. See you!" She left the Dream and placed the truffles in a basket on the front of her bike. With a hand over the Oohoo bulge in her shirt, she pedaled to the tree house.

"Two each? Can Ms. Lenz spare them?" Joshua squinted into the box. "Lots of pretty wrapping, though."

"Don't be silly," Ruth said, grabbing the box from him. "This is something *really* special, Josh. Do you want to try one or can I have yours?"

"No way!" he said.

"Wait, you guys," PJ cut in after releasing Oohoo onto the grass beneath the tree house. "I promised Ms. Lenz I'd be serious about this. Can you split up and try the truffles? Otherwise you're just going to goof off. You have to *savor* the truffles slowly, let them *melt* in your mouth!"

Joshua threw his hand in the air and mimicked PJ's voice, saying, "I'm off to *savor* and *savor*! I'll send my report when I'm done!" He scooped a truffle out of the box, tilted his head back, and dropped it into his mouth.

Ruth rolled her eyes. "Come on, PJ, grab Oohoo. We have work to do."

PJ lifted the owl into her shirt and swung up to the tree house behind Ruth.

Ruth popped a truffle into her own mouth and said, "Omigod. Is this for real?" She sucked in her cheeks and added, "PJ, this is *awesome*. Sweet lemon, keep going all the way to the top of my head! Wow. Tell Ms. Lenz I approve and we'll take any rejects."

"I'll tell her. She's special, Ruth, and you know what? She's so tuned in to owls, she wanted to know why she hadn't heard any at night recently. Have you heard any?" PJ asked.

Ruth pursed her lips and waited until the truffle had totally dissolved before saying, "I don't think so. I wondered why the nights were quiet all of a sudden."

They both looked down at Oohoo bulging out of PJ's shirt and then looked at one another. Something wasn't right. But what?

"Why not take her to the window?" Ruth suggested. "She loves watching sunsets. See if you can get her to open up to you? I'll check on Squirt and Cardy," she added, turning toward their cages.

PJ slid her fingers under the owl's talons and lifted her onto her shoulder.

Above them, the skylight framed the soft pink colors of the sunset like a beautiful painting set into the sloping planks of the ceiling. "Enjoy all those lovely colors, Oohoo," said PJ as the owl nuzzled her cheek. "See how they change from second to second." PJ pointed at the dabs of rose pink sky visible between the curvy, vine-covered branches of the live oak.

Behind them on the big cushions, Squirt played a gymnastic game with Ruth, winding himself around her arms and leaping from one hand to the other. "Nothing wrong with you, my friend." Ruth laughed. She checked Squirt's back leg muscles.

Cardy lifted his brilliant red-plumed head and conical beak and suddenly started to sing, a beautiful *chirpchirpchirp* followed by *pewpewpew*, over and over.

A car backfired outside. Cardy stopped singing. The owl stiffened, ears spiked and sharp, and dug her talons into PJ's shoulder. The tree house was silent for a moment.

PJ kept perfectly still. "Oohoo, it's time you talked to me."

The owl glanced over at Ruth, but she had Cardy on her raised knee and Squirt tumbling about in her hands.

"Talk, Oohoo. You can see Ruth's busy!"

Oohoo listened for a moment, then whispered in PJ's ear, a long hollow sound like wind moving through a tunnel. "I'm safe here."

PJ turned her head so she could whisper in the owl's ear. "Safe?"

"From the owl thief. He sells us to pet stores. He took my chicks. And friends."

PJ jumped up and Oohoo nearly toppled off her shoulder. "Owls aren't pets. Who's stealing them?"

Oohoo stared at the skylight. The sunset was easing from pink into gray streaks. "He's dangerous."

"Who?"

The owl shuddered.

"Oohoo, we know something's going on. Who's stealing owls?"

"The helicopter pilot."

"*Pete?* That's impossible!"

"It's true," Oohoo said.

"But he was so nice. He flew me over the cliffs to find my little bird friend Lemon Pie. . . ." PJ paused. "Oh wow. You mean he uses the helicopter to find baby owls?"

"Ooooh," whispered Oohoo, and the long single note vibrated through PJ's shoulder. Tears rolled out of Oohoo's huge eyes and down her softly mottled feathers.

After a moment, Ruth said, "We need to talk about this, don't we? It's OK. I heard everything." Ruth's gold-flecked gray eyes moved between PJ and Oohoo, and she twirled her pigtail as though trying to figure something out.

Squirt was stretched out along her thigh. Cardy *chirruped* and hopped around her feet.

Oohoo began to rock back and forth.

Ruth gestured to PJ to join her on the pillows. PJ placed one reassuring hand behind Oohoo to steady her as she knelt down.

The older girl folded her arms. "How do we tackle Helicopter Pete?"

"Carefully. I can't let my parents find out," said PJ. "I don't want to give them another reason for an argument."

Ruth had heard that PJ's parents were having problems. "Do you want to talk about it?" she asked.

"Not right now. Let's work out a way of dealing with Helicopter Pete."

"OK, PJ, I hear you. Where does he hang out?"

"I'll ask Mrs. Patel. She'll know," said PJ.

"YO!" Joshua suddenly shouted from below. "I just e-mailed Ms. Lenz. That Lemon Nectar is *dangerous.* When word gets out, she'll have to hire security guards. Folks'll be climbing through her windows to get at the truffles!"

Ruth lifted Squirt off her leg and went to the door. She was just about to give a snide response, but then looked at her twin thoughtfully. "Hey, Josh? Can you free up some of your schedule for the next few days? We may need your camcorder skills."

He blinked up at her. "To video the truffles?"

"No, you moron. We're working on a criminal investigation."

"No kidding! Sounds *hot!*"

"It is!" PJ agreed, joining Ruth at the door. "We start tomorrow, Josh."

Ruth added, "Not a word to Mom and Dad, OK?"

"*Now* you're talking!" He grinned.

PJ eased Oohoo off her shoulder and placed her carefully in her cage. She glanced up at Ruth and said, "Meet me outside Mrs. Patel's house on your bike tomorrow after school?"

☼

When PJ returned home, she left the box of truffles on the kitchen table. She made some excuse to her mom about homework and took a bowl of stir-fried veggies and brown rice up to her room. She needed alone time and didn't want to be in a situation at dinner where her parents argued or asked her too many questions.

She reached for her sketch pad and pastels and began

playing around with colors on the pad, blending and rubbing them with her fingers to try to match the gentle contrasts of merging pinks she'd enjoyed earlier. What lingered in her mind was the image of the skylight framing the sunset like a painting, so she sketched it from memory, complete with the view of curvy branches in the background. She put down the pastels, picked up her dinner, and started to eat it, but soon lost interest and put it to one side. Darkness was settling in. Ms. Lenz had spoken earlier about the silence at night and a sky that was empty of owls.

PJ opened her windows and listened. Nothing. There had to be an easier, faster way of finding out more about the neighborhood owls. She hunted for her flashlight and pulled a dark hoodie over her head. Then she turned on the radio, hoping her parents wouldn't try to talk to her for another hour or two. She could hear the TV in the front room.

PJ scrambled out the window, down a trellis to the grass, and over to Ruth's garden. She scaled the treehouse ladder and took a startled Oohoo from her cage. With Oohoo zipped up inside the hoodie, PJ swung herself down and ran over to Mr. Splitzky's.

"Oohoo," she whispered, edging her way out of view of Mr. Splitzky's windows, all lit up. "You know lots of owls nest in the barn roof. Can you help me find out if anyone's left?"

The owl popped her head above the zipper and started to hoot but PJ shushed her. "Wait, we're not there yet."

Blossom, Mr. Splitzky's dog, met PJ at the gate, happily swishing her long, bushy tail.

"Here, Blossom, good girl, good *girrrrrrl!*" whispered PJ. Luckily the dog knew her so well, she didn't even bark. PJ crunched her way up the granite gravel path, past the hives humming with bees, toward the barn where Mr. Splitzky stored his honey. Blossom trotted close to PJ's heels. Oohoo disappeared deep down inside PJ's shirt so no one would see her, especially the dog.

The barn interior was deliciously fragrant. It took all PJ's willpower not to dip into one of the jars that lined shelves on either side of the door.

She waited until her eyes were fully accustomed to the dim interior. "OK, Oohoo, you can come out now. Where exactly do your owl buddies live?" PJ asked. She squinted up at the dark outlines of crisscross beams and rafters.

Oohoo's head popped out under PJ's chin. "Unzip me, PJ."

PJ placed a cautionary hand on Blossom's head to keep her from barking as Oohoo hopped onto PJ's shoulder and flew off. The owl circled the interior of the barn a couple of times before soaring upward, making gentle hoots as she ascended. PJ lost sight of her but didn't want to shine the flashlight around in case she frightened anything else that might be nesting in the beams. Blossom sniffed the air and sat down obediently by PJ's side.

Within minutes, Oohoo came swooping back to PJ's shoulder. "They've all gone, PJ. Monkey Face, Tyto, and the rest, just as I thought," the owl said sadly. "They haven't been here for a *looooong* time. I can tell."

"Oh, that's too bad. Why not squat in their space?"

"Squat?" asked Oohoo, head to one side.

"Just move in and keep the place warm in case they come back."

Oohoo was silent for a moment. "PJ, I'm a *flammulated* owl. We live in trees. Monkey Face and Tyto are common barn owls with white faces all heart-shaped. Not like *me*. We're friends, but we don't *live* the same way."

"Oh," said PJ.

The owl added, "*They* live in old buildings, caves, and trees. *We* like hollow branches. Think of my colors, PJ." She pointed a tip of her wing at her madly mottled and striped collection of rusts, browns, and grays. "You wouldn't notice me in a tree, would you?"

"I'd notice you anywhere, Oohoo."

"Oh, come on, PJ! I hoot. Barn owls hiss. We eat insects. They eat mice and things."

"I thought all you owls ate the same things."

Oohoo rolled her large brown eyes in exasperation.

Undaunted, PJ asked, "You think they escaped because they were scared? Can we look somewhere else?"

"No. The nights are silent, just as Ms. Lenz said. I've listened. Helicopter Pete must have trapped them with the others." Oohoo sighed.

"Then help us find them, Oohoo. Don't give up. You saw it happen. Which direction did Pete take?"

Oohoo nodded toward the west.

Suddenly, Blossom began to bark loudly.

"Oh wow," said PJ. "Hop into my hoodie again. Quickly, Oohoo. I think Blossom's warning us!"

PJ was right. Just as she ducked behind some old planks of wood with Oohoo, the door swung open. Mr. Splitzky stood there in a beam from the sensor lights. Blossom immediately turned in the opposite direction and began digging frantically under a pile of burlap. "Come on, Bloss, girl!" Mr. Splitzky said. "It's probably a mouse and you'll never catch it! C'mon, let's go walkies!" Blossom bounded toward the door and followed her owner outside.

PJ and Oohoo peeped out of a broken beam in the barn wall and waited until Mr. Splitzky and Blossom were well out of sight. *Good dog,* thought PJ. She didn't want to have to explain herself to Mr. Splitzky at *this* time of night!

It was velvety dark when they ventured outside, tiptoeing around close to the barn to avoid the sensor light. PJ walked back to Ruth's. Oohoo was asleep by the time PJ climbed up to the tree house and placed her in the cage.

As she reached her own home, PJ could hear her parents arguing loudly in the kitchen. For once she felt relieved, because she knew they wouldn't notice her climbing the trellis up to her bedroom window. When they peeked in her door later, she pretended to be fast asleep.

Just before dawn, she tiptoed downstairs for something to drink and found two separate messages chalked up on the board in the kitchen. Her mother wrote, "Truffles are divine." Her father wrote, "Candies are far too sweet."

CHAPTER 7

helicopter pete

PJ sat in the front window munching apples and cheese when she got home from school, and then called Mrs. Patel.

"Hi, Mrs. Patel. Any idea where I can find Helicopter Pete?"

"Oh, no problem, child," replied Mrs. Patel. "I just saw him land at the helipad. He usually pops into the Buzz coffee shop after flying. Why?"

"Oh, um, Ruth and I wanted to talk to Pete about something," PJ said. "It's a new project."

"A new project," Mrs. Patel said slowly. "Hmmm. I wonder what you are up to now?"

"Up to? Come on, Mrs. Patel. You know me better than that!" she said.

"I can see you through the window, PJ. Meet me outside?"

As PJ joined her in the street, Ruth came hurtling around the corner on her bicycle and skidded dizzily to a stop.

Mrs. Patel jumped out of the way. "Now, girls, I don't want you playing hijinks on your bikes like this. You set a bad example for the younger kids!"

"We won't. Bye, Mrs. Patel," said PJ, and she ran to get her own bike before Mrs. Patel could say anything else.

The two girls cycled off in convoy. Once they were out of earshot, PJ told Ruth about her adventure with Oohoo in Mr. Splitzky's barn.

Ruth sucked in her breath. "Wow. You took a chance. You rock, PJ!"

"Just call me PJ 'Chance' Picklelime," said PJ, feeling proud at earning Ruth's approval.

Within ten minutes they caught sight of Pete's blue-green chopper on the helipad, like a huge dragonfly glinting in the afternoon sun. And just as Mrs. Patel had assured them, tall Pete with his balding head and stringy circle of hair was sitting outside the nearby Buzz, enjoying a tall latte

and a cinnamon bun. He rose as they approached. "Come and join me, girls. What can I get you?"

"Orange juice," said Ruth.

"Nothing," said PJ.

"We'll both have orange juice, thanks, Pete!" Ruth cut in. As they parked and locked their bikes by the curb, she whispered, "Cool it, PJ. Pretend this is a social visit. Otherwise he'll get suspicious!"

They pulled up chairs opposite Pete, and Ruth casually asked him what he was up to these days, now that that bird rescue was over.

"Oh, this and that," he said, wiping speckles of cinnamon bun icing off his cheeks. "Picking up computer supplies, my regular job. Sometimes the coast guard needs backup. You girls are welcome to fly with me as long as I get the OK from your folks. Or if Mrs. Patel joins us like last time, PJ!"

PJ said nothing.

Ruth leaned forward on her elbows. "Pete, we need your help," she said.

"We heard something at school that makes us *really* unhappy. You fly all over the place, so you see a lot of things from the air we don't see from our bicycles. Right, PJ?"

"Oh. Right," PJ said. Unlike Ruth, who was playing the innocent card, PJ could barely look at Pete. She hated to think about what he might have done to Tyto, Monkey Face, and Oohoo's chicks.

"A couple of kids told one of our teachers that someone was stealing owls," Ruth went on, widening her gold-flecked gray eyes. She flicked her long pigtail away from her ear. "This jerk was trapping them to sell to pet stores. Have you ever heard anything so *awful*?"

Pete stared at her for a second, then made a great show of shaking his head. "The things people do. Which kid told you this?"

"The whole group was discussing it and someone's contacted Animal Planet," she fibbed, nudging PJ under the table. "We wondered if you had seen anything."

Pete leaned back, eyes darting between the two girls, and folded his arms. "I haven't. Kids shouldn't be involved. Maybe I should go talk to your teacher, see how I can help?"

PJ and Ruth exchanged glances, then PJ said tightly, "Our teacher told us to get involved."

Pete ran a hand over his balding crown and said, "Girls, I have to leave you. My head'll start blistering under the sun soon. Hey, I'll keep my eyes open, OK? I promise. Anything I find out I'll pass along to Mrs. Patel."

Pete rose and strode off toward his dragonfly blue-green chopper on the helipad. Ruth and PJ watched in silence as he climbed inside the cockpit and seemed to search for something.

"You nearly blew it," said Ruth, sipping her juice. "You have to learn to be cool when you try to trick someone on the opposite side, like using fancy footwork in soccer. The important thing is never to show anger."

"I can't help it." PJ waited until Pete jumped down off the chopper and disappeared into the helipad office before asking, "OK. What now?"

"He knows something's up. I'm going to call the animal hotline from a public phone, disguise and deepen my voice, pretend I'm from France. 'I 'ave im-por-tant news *pour vous* about an owl thief,'" she said, exaggerating a French accent. "They'll *never* know it's me!"

"Oh, c'mon, Ruth, they record those calls and run one of those voice-matching machines with all the zigzag lines if there's a problem. Maybe we *should* start dropping hints around school? You know how word spreads."

"I don't think we have that sort of time. We need to move. Fast! I'm going to hit the Internet, see which pet shops offer exotic birds," she added.

"Hmmm," PJ said thoughtfully. "Oohoo said barn owls eat mice, so whoever trapped them must have a fresh source. You should Google pet shops that sell birds and mice."

"Good point, PJ. Let's touch base later. We'll brainstorm a rescue plan my twin, Spielberg the Second, can catch on his camcorder!"

"That's who you meant by Animal Planet?" PJ grinned and adjusted her bike helmet.

"Oh, well, local media first. Then who knows who'll pick up the story?"

※

PJ's father met her at the front door. He was not in a good mood.

"PJ, how many times have I told you *not* to feed birds on your window ledge?" he said. "It's *disgusting*. And unhygienic. The ledge is covered with bird droppings stuck with feathers!"

"I'm not feeding birds there, Dad," PJ said truthfully.

"Well, someone must be feeding them. *Our* bedroom window ledge doesn't look like that."

"Birds enjoy flying around my windows. They don't

enjoy . . ." Her words trailed off and she looked up at her father.

"Don't enjoy what?"

"Dad, if I can hear you and Mom arguing, so can the birds."

Mr. Picklelime's face turned beet red. "What have I told you about snooping outside our bedroom door?"

"I don't snoop," PJ said angrily. "I can hear you argue through the walls. Come on, Dad. Don't treat me like a baby."

"PJ, we need to talk. *After* you clean your window ledge." He went into the kitchen and handed her a bucket, brush, cloth, and citrus all-purpose cleanser.

PJ took the cleaning things without a word and went up to her room. She closed the door behind her and flung open her windows. Cawing seagulls wheeled around noisily above the house as though waiting for a sweep of fish to rise and roll over in a huge wave. She held a finger to her lips and scrubbed the ledge. When it was clean, PJ made a welcoming gesture to the gulls.

As if on cue, two of them swooped down.

"Hey, thanks, PJ," the larger one said. "It's been kinda skanky around here." He tilted a wing down toward the ledge.

PJ was startled. "How do you know my name?"

"I'm Big Gull, at your service." He bowed with a flourish. "My sister, Little Gull, and I were fostered by your Lemon Pie," he said, and nodded sideways at the smaller gull beside him. "Our friends call us BG and LG."

PJ whooped with joy and reached out to stroke their soft white bellies and polka-dot tails. "Oh great! Messenger Gull sent you, right? But shhh. Don't give me away. My dad's *real* mad."

"So we heard," they chorused.

"Guys, tell your friends to lower the volume around the windows, OK?"

"You got it, PJ," said Little Gull. "We'll tell the others. Hey, any more Messenger Gull b-mails from Lemon Pie?"

PJ shook her head sadly. "It's OK. He has to explore the world in his own way now. He doesn't need me."

"*We* need you, PJ!" Big Gull nuzzled her hand with his beak.

"Yeah, right, BG. I think you just want to be spoiled!" PJ smiled at one gull and then at the other and silently thanked Messenger Gull for prompting the visit. Talk about timing! Perhaps they could help with the rescue plan? "Listen, you guys, I have a favor to ask," she said. "Fly inland and check out some pet stores on any main street to the west of here. They could be near a helipad. Can you find out which ones are selling owls and mice?"

"Owls? We don't do owls," said Little Gull.

"Hold it," said Big Gull. "Why, PJ?"

"Haven't you noticed how quiet it is around here at night?"

"How would we know? We're day birds," said Little Gull.

"Why's it always about you, LG?" BG snapped.

PJ held up her hand. "We're in crisis and need your help," she said, and told them why.

"We're on it, PJ," said BG, glaring at LG.

"Thanks, guys. Now off you go. I need to talk to my dad. This is serious."

"Oooh, serious! Don't forget to 'drop' some mixed seeds in the garden, PJ. Now *that's* serious! Right, BG?" said Little Gull.

"Right, LG," Big Gull replied.

"Freeloaders, that's all you are! Go on. Check in with me later!"

Big Gull and Little Gull made a great show of

pretending to fall off the ledge before they swooped and *caw-cawed* away from the window in wide circles.

"PJ, who are you talking to in the street?" Mr. Picklelime asked from outside her door.

PJ pulled in quickly, shut the windows, and pretended not to hear. "OK, Dad, everything's clean! Come in and look!" she called out cheerfully.

He opened the door. His eyes swept the window ledge and the sky beyond, but he made no comment. "We'll talk in the kitchen, PJ," he said.

PJ followed him downstairs and helped him chop Costa Rican pineapple, bananas, and mangoes to throw into the blender for smoothies. Mr. Picklelime filled two tall glasses with balloons painted all over them. PJ stuck thick spiral glass straws into the drinks.

"PJ, your mom and I are going through some changes."

"Is that why you argue?" PJ asked.

"It's . . . more complicated than that," her dad said, taking a quick sip.

"Why?"

"I don't want to go there."

"Dad, you and Mom seem to think I'm too young to

know what's going on. I hate it. Does everyone believe I'm either deaf or stupid? You walk away from us all the time and Mom spouts poetry when she's upset."

Mr. Picklelime sat back and stirred his smoothie. "I can't blame your mom for needing space. She's going away for a while to do some graduate training in counseling."

"You mean *Mom's* moving out?"

"Not quite. She'll be home every weekend."

PJ pushed her smoothie away and sat back. Outside the kitchen window, the gulls formed a zigzag line of tiny black V shapes, like musical notes in the graying sky. She listened in her heart to their carefree *caw-cawing* and the comforting link to Lemon Pie that call meant now. She longed to fly away with them.

Her dad was trying to make reassuring comments about "not worrying" and "bringing work home" and "fun evenings cooking together or sending out for pizza," but PJ didn't want to hear it.

Then Mr. Picklelime said, "I can't blame *you* for spending less time at home recently. It's not just this animal rescue fad, is it?"

"It's *not* a fad. It's something I really want to do."

"You're neglecting your homework," he said.

"I'm not. What are you and Mom arguing about?" PJ asked.

"That's private. Between us."

"Dad, please." PJ placed both hands flat on the kitchen table. "This isn't a talk show. Half the kids in my class have parents with problems. You think we don't pick up on these things? I want to hear everything from you. Not *pssst pssst pssst* gossipy bits from the neighborhood!"

He shrugged. "There's nothing to tell. Mom and I disagree on some things." Mr. Picklelime sipped more smoothie and stared at his daughter. "PJ, don't push it."

The front door opened and slammed shut. Mrs. Picklelime poked her head around the kitchen door, said something like, "Oh," and disappeared.

❀

Later PJ called Ruth from her room. "Hi, Ruth. You knew my parents were having problems, didn't you?"

"I heard things, sure. But I felt you didn't want to talk about it yesterday. I'm so sorry."

"Thanks. It's tough." PJ paused and bit her lip. Her parents didn't laugh together anymore. That's why she didn't hang out at home so much. "I like spending time with Mrs. Patel or you and the birds," PJ said. She started to sketch Big Gull and Little Gull frolicking in the sky.

Ruth said, "PJ, you're part of the tree-house family. You're not alone."

PJ didn't reply.

"You still there?" Ruth asked.

"Sure."

"Are they arguing a lot?"

"More and more."

"My advice? Cover your ears. Remember you're not the reason they're arguing."

The kindness in Ruth's voice was comforting, but PJ didn't really want to go into details. "I don't want you to think I'm being disloyal to my parents," she explained.

"I don't, PJ. You could never be disloyal."

Both girls were silent for a few moments. "Feel up to talking about the owls?" Ruth asked, then she said, "I could call later if you like?"

"No, I'm OK. I want to hear what you found out."

"I Googled pet stores in a radius of twenty miles and came across a couple of possibilities. Wings and Tweety Birds."

"Great! I've just made some new gull friends and sent

them wheeling around to see what they can discover, too."

"What a team, PJ! Let's compare notes tomorrow," Ruth suggested. "Whoa, Cardy just flew off. A lady cardinal was batting her eyelids at him outside the window." She chuckled.

PJ smiled. "Cardy won't go too far away. Unlike Lemon Pie."

"Hmmm, we'll have to keep our eyes open for little Cardinellas, won't we?"

After she hung up the phone, PJ closed her eyes and conjured up the sights and sounds of Ruth's garden. She imagined the red splashes Cardy would make flying from branch to branch and *chirruping* after his soft brown lady love with her red plume. She pictured the lawn after a downpour of rain, covered with white rain lilies. There were huge, old sprawling live oaks, pecan trees, and hedges of sweet-smelling honeysuckle. Circular beds of tall, deep pink coneflowers waved in the wind. Water bubbled out of a graceful fountain sculpture of a girl carrying an earthenware pot. Frogs croaked nearby. When she opened her eyes again, she quickly sketched the garden in pastels.

PJ's thoughts also drifted over to Mrs. Patel's garden. Then she looked out the window. Her mother hadn't started to plant anything yet as she usually did in spring. PJ hadn't even noticed until this moment. The yellow Lady Banks rosebush was beginning to drop its petals to the soft earth below. It had been a long time since its blooms flourished when Lemon Pie hid there. Even the lawn needed some care. If her mom was going away, perhaps Mrs. Patel would help her? She knew her dad wasn't all that interested in the garden, except to complain when the friendly gulls pooped on the lawn.

"PJ?" her mom called out.

PJ opened her bedroom door. "I'm here, Mom!"

"Let's go for a walk, honey," her mom said from the stairs. "Mrs. Patel's invited us over for one of her special curries later."

PJ reached for a red fleecy pullover. A chilly, salty breeze had moved in from the sea, the sort of breeze that matted and tightened her growing crop of black curls. She joined her mom in the road. "Is Dad coming?"

"No. I hear you and your dad have talked."

PJ nodded and shivered and dug her hands into her pockets.

"I want to go back to work, PJ. I need to do some courses before renewing my counseling license. It won't take long."

As they started to walk, PJ ran her hands across the top of a huge rosemary bush that bordered the sidewalk and then raised her fingertips to her nose to inhale the essence of the sprigs combined with sea salt. "Aren't you really going away because you and Dad argue a lot?" PJ asked.

Mrs. Picklelime shook her head. "We just need a little space."

"When are you going?"

"Soon."

"Oh." PJ listened. Breezes moved Ms. Naguri's bamboo chimes on one side of the road, harmonizing with the deep resonance of Mrs. Patel's metal chimes on the other side. Sometimes, depending which way the wind blew in from the sea, PJ could enjoy their comforting sounds at night. She loved them.

PJ realized her mom was talking to her.

"I wish things were different, but I really need this time and space for me. Even if your dad and I didn't argue. Do you understand?"

PJ nodded. "I do, Mom." She watched her mother's denim sneakers and her own fire-engine red sneakers move together along the sidewalk. "I want to be an architect so I can design funky tree houses or barns or houseboats and gardens for people and animals so no one needs to ask anyone for space."

Mrs. Picklelime smiled at her daughter. "You do that. Find a soul mate with wonderfully crazy ideas just like yours!"

PJ slipped her arm around her mom's waist. "What happens when you stop being soul mates? Do moms and dads just stop loving one another? You know, just like that?" she asked, snapping her fingers.

"Now the poet Keats would say, '*At a touch sweet Pleasure melteth, Like to bubbles when rain pelteth,*' " whispered her mom. Then, "PJ, you know far too much for a girl of your age."

"Oh, Mom, *please!*" PJ said irritably. They stopped talking as they reached Mrs. Patel's gate and followed one another along her pebble path to the front door. The evening air was getting even chillier. PJ was glad to step into the warm kitchen with its fragrantly spicy smells and a lovely tablecloth patterned with hummingbirds.

Mr. Patel was a systems analyst and working late, so it was just the three of them—a "girls' night out," as Mrs. Picklelime said.

Mrs. Patel placed steaming bowls of orange *daal*, mixed-vegetable curry, and saffron rice on the table. She warmed up thin, crisp *papadum* and spread all PJ's favorite little side dishes around. There were bowls of sliced banana, grated coconut, lemon chutney, tomato, and yogurt with cucumber.

Before they ate, Mrs. Patel reached out and clasped PJ's and Mrs. Picklelime's hands and said, "Peace to our food and our friendship."

"Always." PJ smiled. "What a feast!"

"Shanti, you spoil us," said Mrs. Picklelime.

Once they started eating and bowls crisscrossed the table, PJ asked, "Mrs. Patel, are you and Mr. Patel soul mates?"

Her mom stopped sprinkling coconut over her curry. "PJ, that's very personal."

Shanti Patel threw back her head and laughed, a wonderfully musical laugh. "No, of course it isn't! Oh, child. We were married very young. What did we know about soul mates in those days? But we were good friends, you know? We were at school together." She thought for a minute. "You can't be soul mates without being good friends. Why do you ask?"

PJ and her mom exchanged quick glances. Mrs. Patel picked up on this, eyes moving kindly between mother and daughter. "Child, sometimes people marry for all sorts of reasons without being soul mates," she said. "You're very young, PJ. But not too young to learn some good life lessons from this. Friends and partners can grow in different directions and become closer. Or grow apart. Now, come, we're getting too serious! Shall I heat more *papadum*?"

Later, when PJ and Mrs. Patel were alone for a moment, PJ asked her for some gardening advice for their skimpy flower beds and lawn.

"Of course, child. Come tomorrow afternoon to my greenhouse and we'll get cracking. We can plan lovely surprises for your mom when she comes home every weekend!"

As her mother returned to the kitchen, PJ looked up and realized her mom had also talked privately to Mrs. Patel, otherwise how did Mrs. Patel know she was leaving?

Mrs. Patel smiled at her reassuringly and said, "Reach into the fridge, PJ. I made your favorite, mango ice cream, for dessert!"

The moon was high and hazy through the salty night air by the time Mrs. Picklelime and PJ left the warmth of Mrs. Patel's kitchen to go home. They were both sleepy, but it had been a lovely evening they knew they would remember for a long time.

"I'll miss you, Mom," PJ said as her mother unlocked the front door. "Even when I don't see you I know you're around. Soon you won't be."

"Remember we'll see each other every five days, honey. That's not too long for us to be apart, is it?"

CHAPTER 8

operation owl rescue

When **PJ left school** the next afternoon, the air was fresh and sparkling and the sky was a sharp blue, free of the heavy sea mists of the evening before.

She joined Mrs. Patel in her greenhouse and selected some tiny cherry tomatoes from clusters of sturdy vines. PJ couldn't resist popping a few of them into her mouth and snapping the skins between her teeth. "Mmmm," she said, juice trickling from her lips. "They're like fruit. *Soooo* sweet, Mrs. Patel!"

"Pick as many as you like. Here, fill this," she said, handing PJ a basket. "Put the tomatoes in a beautiful bowl in the middle of your kitchen table to light up the room. Come, I'll help you create your own garden. Let's start you off with some sweet-smelling herbs." She selected pots of basil, thyme, parsley, and oregano and placed them in a plastic tray. When PJ didn't react, she added, "Be strong, PJ. Trust me, child. I know what it's like when parents go through a rough patch. Work extra hard at school. Make your room into your den and pin up more of your lovely artwork, so you always have a little place where you feel good. Keep working with birds and animals. They're great teachers."

"I know," PJ said.

As they carried their overflowing baskets of tomatoes into the kitchen and rinsed them in filtered rainwater, Mrs. Patel told PJ about the ways some animals could predict earthquakes or volcanic eruptions or other disasters.

"When they had an earthquake in China, the streets were jumping with frogs and all the ponds suddenly emptied. Birds disappeared from the skies. Cows threw themselves against fences," said Mrs. Patel. "PJ, make a note of *everything* you are learning now from animals. They make you more observant."

"My dad said my work with animals was just a fad," PJ said.

Mrs. Patel chuckled. "Child, don't worry. Sometimes our parents don't understand us! My father couldn't understand why I collected seeds from pods and grew them on windowsills in different types of soil to see which grew faster in which soil, which light, or which warm spot. When I tried to grow roses in a new color by attaching a crimson rose to a yellow rose, he said botany was a waste of time for a girl."

PJ tried to imagine Mrs. Patel as a young girl. All the wonderfully abundant vines of bougainvillea she could see peeping through the kitchen window seemed different now. Mrs. Patel was more than just a good gardener. She had *lived* gardening for years! If Mrs. Patel could achieve her dreams in spite of a difficult father, so could she.

"Come, child. Time I taught you how to compost!" said Mrs. Patel.

They returned to the garden, carrying containers of tomato stalks, veggie peels from the night before, and a mountain of tea leaves. They tipped the containers into one of the tumbler compost bins by the back fence and tossed a layer of hedge clippings over the bits. After replacing the lid, PJ spun the tumbler bin around on its frame like a trapeze artist.

PJ wrinkled her nose. "Mrs. Patel, p'yew!" she said. "This must stink in summer!"

Mrs. Patel laughed. "It breaks down fast in summer, you wait and see. Now, look in the other bin."

PJ twisted the lid off the second tumbler and peeked inside. Freshly composted, loamy, rich-looking soil filled the bin almost to the rim.

Mrs. Patel reached in for a handful, raised it to her nostrils, and said, "Hmmm. *Perfect.* This is how good compost should feel and smell, PJ. Open your hands."

PJ opened both hands but couldn't quite match Mrs. Patel's excitement, except she loved the feeling of the crumbly soil. "So, leaves and clippings and veggie peels all break down to *this*?" she asked.

"Oh yes. With heat, of course, and a little moisture. When you cut your crop of hair again, you can add your curls to the mix. It breaks down well and keeps animals away. Now run and get the wheelbarrow, gloves, and spades, child. We'll take some lovely compost across to your garden."

They wheeled the barrow of compost, potted herbs, and young tomato and jasmine plants from Mrs. Patel's greenhouse, and a basket of cherry tomatoes, across the road to the Picklelimes'.

"PJ, what's going on with that veggie patch?" Mrs. Patel asked. She shook her head at a forlorn corner covered with straggly carrot and potato tops.

"I think we collected the last of the carrots and potatoes weeks ago," said PJ. Compared with the gardens of Mrs. Patel and Ruth, the Picklelimes' garden seemed neglected. Their live oak and pecan trees weren't as old, sprawly, and exciting as those in Ruth's garden.

"We'll tackle the veggie patch another time," said Mrs. Patel tactfully. "Let's get a line of herbs organized in the troughs by the kitchen door first of all."

They cleaned debris and old leaves out of the troughs and filled them with loamy composted soil mixed with garden soil. In one trough they planted rows of basil with the tomato plants. Then they mixed thyme, basil, oregano, curly parsley, and Italian parsley in the other troughs.

"Fetch some rainwater, PJ," said Mrs. Patel. PJ ran over to the rain collection barrel and filled a bucket. "Don't forget to water everything thoroughly each day for a week," Mrs. Patel continued. "The herbs will reward you. Not only will they give you freshness for soups and pastas, but on a warm summer evening they'll release their lovely smell for hours. Especially the basil."

"Where shall we plant this, Mrs. Patel?" PJ asked as she reached for the climbing jasmine.

"I thought you might like that on your window ledge, child."

PJ hesitated, trying to imagine the gulls' reaction if she cluttered their landing pad! "I think I'd like it climbing up the trellis," she said.

"Good choice. Some other time you can go from window to window and look out at the garden. I'll follow you around outside and you can tell me where to mark the best views for new beds. We'll make a note of shady areas and sunny areas. Then we can choose special flowers and flowering shrubs."

"So we'll always have pretty views?"

"Right, and we'll choose plants that flourish in different seasons."

"Mrs. Patel?"

"Yes, child?"

"Do you find soul mates through your flowers?" PJ asked. She loaded the spade into the empty wheelbarrow and pulled off her gardening gloves.

"PJ, soul mates don't *look* for one another. They *find* one another. Soul mates don't always marry. They don't need to." Mrs. Patel paused as they wheeled the barrow back across the street. "Still, it helps if your life partner is a soul mate. Make sense?"

PJ pushed open the Patels' gate. "Are we soul mates, Mrs. Patel?" she asked.

"Child, we're kindred spirits. You and Ruth are also kindred spirits. That's more, much more, than just being good friends. It means we share thoughts and understandings without a need for explanations." After a minute, Mrs. Patel added, "You need to wait a few more years, dear PJ, before you experience a true soul mate. Now stop worrying! Start making a list of all your favorite flowers and colors for those window views!"

☀

"Hey, PJ! *Niiiiiiice* herbs you planted for us!" The gulls *rat-a-tat-tatted* PJ's window before sunrise. She sat up. Big Gull and Little Gull flapped up and down outside in the blustery wind, an agitated dance of gray and white feathers, dark wings, and black polka-dot tails against a perfect backdrop of a slate gray sky.

PJ flung open the windows and waved them inside. "Shhh, keep it down, guys," she said. "Those herbs are off-limits, you scroungers!"

"Not so fast! Good news. We found a store selling wild birds," said Big Gull.

"*Go, gulls!* What's it called?" PJ shook a bag of nuts and seeds onto her window seat.

The two seagulls began pecking furiously before Big Gull lifted his head and said between mouthfuls, "Tweety Birds."

"So it's Tweety's!" said PJ. That was one of the names Ruth had found on the Internet! "Guys, we're moving into action. I need another favor."

"Oooh, a favor," said Big Gull. "That'll cost you, PJ. I mean, nuts and seeds will do for now. Talk to us. Then we'll deal."

PJ quickly outlined a plan to rescue the owls from the pet store.

"Are you kidding us? Owls aren't our friends!" said Little Gull.

"C'mon, BG, LG. Don't be like that! This is community action! I'd send every bird I knew out to rescue *you* guys if you were in danger," PJ replied.

"Yeah, right. Send some friendly hawks our way, PJ, why don't you? They *eat* other birds!" said Little Gull.

"LG, no one expects a pint-size like you to go face

down a bunch of *hawks*!" said BG, rolling his eyes. "Quit filling your beak with seeds. Can I talk to you?"

LG swallowed and waddled closer. The two gulls huddled together, raising wing tips to their beaks so PJ wouldn't overhear their private conversation. Finally, they turned back to PJ.

"It's a deal," said BG.

"You guys rock, you really do!" PJ said.

"We'd like to try some of that deluxe birdseed we've seen delivered in purple plastic bags to the health food stores," said BG. "They never stack the bags outside for us to peck open."

"Yeah, real inconsiderate." LG nodded.

"You got it. Tap on my windows when you have news for me. If I'm not here, I'll be at Ruth's tree house." PJ told them how to fly there. "I'll keep that special birdseed on me for you, OK?" she added.

"OK. But we can't promise anything," said LG.

"Do your best?" PJ said.

"We will, kiddo," BG assured her. "Hey. We'll bring the Gull Gang along."

"Gull Gang?" PJ frowned.

"Just a bunch of gulls that hang out with us," BG said, winking at LG.

"No violence. Agreed?"

BG tapped her cheek with his wing, tilted his head, and said, "Violence? You know us better than that, PJ. Let's go, LG. We've got work to do!"

"Plan of action: late afternoon, just before closing time, OK?" said PJ.

"You got it." BG nodded wisely.

The gulls spent the next few minutes pecking up the rest of the seeds.

PJ watched them hop from the window seat onto the window ledge and swoop off in their characteristic cheeky way. They dipped and tumbled in the wind and twirled around one another, putting on a big show for her before soaring high and flying off toward the coast.

PJ reached for her phone and speed-dialed Ruth's number. She left a brief voice mail. "Dandelion juice bar next to Tweety's. Just before closing time. Tell Joshua."

-☀-

"OK, kids," BG said to members of the Gull Gang lined up on a large, flat rock that jutted out of the cliff's edge. "Here's the deal."

The "gang" of twelve gulls hunched together so BG

didn't have to squawk over the blustery wind. BG and LG were battle-scarred heroes to them all, because of their tough reputation for tackling hawks. Below them, the choppy, white-crested waves chased one another relentlessly, churning sand and seaweed onto the beach.

"Just over there"—BG nodded inland—"in the next town of Primrose-on-Sea, there's a pet store on the main street between a drugstore and a juice bar. Can't miss it. It's called Tweety Birds. Tweety's owner needs to be taught a little lesson. For selling owls stolen from *our* 'hood."

The gulls began talking at once. "Selling stolen local owls?" "No way!" "Scumbag." "We'll give him Tweety, Big Gull." "You mean folks actually buy owls?"

BG held up his wings for silence. "Kids, your full attention. All I want you to do is create a whole lotta noise outside Tweety's windows to divert the owner's attention. Leave the rest up to LG and me, OK?"

"Let's roll, BG, LG! Let's *go*!"

"Hey hey hey, wait, kids! Not so fast. We need to swoop down just before closing time when Mr. Tweety's tired. And guys? Hold your fire until then, if you can."

"OK, BG," said the Gull Gang's leader, Loud Laugh, *caw-caw-cawing* up to his reputation.

And so the dozen of them set off later in convoy

over to Primrose-on-Sea, following closely behind BG and LG.

Red streaks of dusk were beginning to spread across the sky, tinging the bank of gray clouds that dimmed the late-afternoon light. Some stores had closed on Main Street. Shoppers dwindled as folks hurried home for dinner.

The timing was perfect.

To the joy of PJ, Ruth, and Joshua, who sat in the bay window of the Dandelion, innocently sipping fresh watermelon juice, the gulls swooped within inches of Tweety's window next door.

And what a sight! They hovered in midflight, wings beating madly. Then they turned around on cue so their tail feathers faced the window.

Joshua rushed out with his camcorder.

SPLAT. Spppplaaaat, squirt, squelch, splat, splat, splat echoed up and down Main Street. Seagull droppings hit the windows and ran down in thick, oozy streaks. No one could even see inside.

"*YES!*" shouted PJ and Ruth, high-fiving in the Dandelion. Joshua gave them a quick thumbs-up. Then he crouched down and zoomed in.

Mr. Tweety ran out waving his arms. "Bug off, you

disgusting seagulls! *BUG OFF*, I say!" But the gulls swooped down over his head. *Splat splat splat*, all over him. Joshua jumped to the side to avoid being hit.

BG and LG immediately flew in the open door and pecked open a line of cages. There wasn't time to go from cage to cage looking for the owls. So they cawed, *"Barn owls and anyone else from the 'hood. Go, just go. GO!"*

Within seconds the store was filled with escaping birds of all colors, sizes, and shapes.

Splashed with bird droppings, Mr. Tweety struggled to get through the door, but the Gull Gang beat him back into the street. Joshua ducked as the birds came flapping out and tilted his tiny camcorder to video them from below. He swung around to focus on Mr. Tweety, who stood there, hands covering his face.

"Freedom, guys, FREEEEE-DOM!" Loud Laugh shouted. The sky blackened above Mr. Tweety's head as more of the captive birds escaped. They hovered for a moment and then soared skyward. Way up, they split ranks, some going east, others going west.

Joshua chased them around the next corner, to catch the birds until they became dots in the sky. Then he ran to the next block to wait for Ruth and PJ by the bike rack.

PJ, Ruth, and other customers rolled about in the bay

window of the Dandelion, laughing hysterically. Crowds began to gather outside.

A police car pulled up at the curb. Officer Julie Dolan hung out and shouted, "Mr. Tweety, what's going on?"

"I was attacked by a bunch of seagulls," he yelled.

"Seagulls?" She glanced upward. The gray and pink sky was empty. She drove off, shaking her head. Mr. Tweety stumbled inside.

Ruth and PJ left the Dandelion and mingled in the crowds, ooohing and wowing for a few moments before racing off to join Joshua. The three took side streets to the nearest Internet cafe and uploaded Joshua's clips onto the Web sites of the local media before cycling home at top speed.

the moonbow

"Pssst. Yo, PJ?" Big Gull *tap-tap-tapped* on her window, peering inside in the dusk. But PJ wasn't home.

"She's probably in Ruth's tree house," Little Gull suggested. "C'mon, BG, let's hop over there."

Together they flew off toward the tree house. It was lit up like a beacon in the sprawling live oaks. They flapped and *caw-cawed* outside, knowing that no one minded weird birds flying in and out of the tree house at all hours. PJ noticed them and flung open the window. "Come in, guys!"

They hopped inside and swaggered about. PJ and the twins clapped and cheered loudly. The trio sat there on the cushions with Oohoo and Squirt, watching local news clips on Ruth's laptop and enjoying thick slices of carrot cake. Ruth turned the laptop around so the gulls could see themselves.

"WooooHOO," said LG and BG. They high-fived their wing tips.

"Josh, great work. Look at Tweety covered with bird droppings!" yelled LG.

"And we *mean* bird droppings," said BG. "Seagull, owl, parakeet, canary, you name it."

"There go Monkey Face and Tyto and some other white-faced barn owls," Oohoo said, watching the laptop with wide eyes. "Can you believe this?"

"Nothing to it," said BG. He waved a wing dismissively. "Can't remember how many owls flew out."

"Plenty," said LG.

Joshua switched to another news Web site. They watched the entire sequence again, including the final clip, when Officer Dolan pulled up in the police car.

Oohoo hopped off PJ's shoulder onto the open window ledge and cocked her head to one side. She lifted one wing and said, "Shhh . . ."

Ruth turned down the sound.

They all listened carefully but couldn't hear the

characteristic *sssssss* of the barn owls outside. "Too early," said Oohoo with a peek up at the darkening sky. She looked at PJ, at Ruth, at the gulls, and back to PJ.

"Go on, Oohoo," said PJ. "Go and look for them if you like. We'll be here for a while."

"I'll leave a window open for you, Oohoo. Come back anytime." Ruth nodded reassuringly.

Still the owl hesitated.

Ruth went to the window and lifted Oohoo into the bowl of her hands. "Go. Make sure Monkey Face and Tyto are OK. Otherwise bring them back here with you."

She opened her hands. Oohoo dipped, winged upward, and flew off with a loud, indignant hoot. The twins and PJ watched her disappear between the dark branches. Ruth glanced at PJ's worried expression and said, "It's OK, kiddo. Oohoo'll be OK."

"I guess so," said PJ. "Thanks, Ruth. I don't think I could just drop her like that!"

"Sometimes that's the only thing to do," said Ruth.

"Way to go!" shouted Big Gull. "PJ, where's that special birdseed you promised? We're two hungry gulls after all that hard work!"

PJ dug in her pockets for a couple of ziplock bags she had filled up in advance.

Squirt jumped up on the window ledge and joined the gulls. He took a pawful of seeds and nibbled them. The gulls pounced on the rest greedily.

Joshua reached for his tiny camcorder and swiveled toward the animals. "Great shot," he said. "You don't often see gulls and squirrels together like this!"

"Don't get too close," Ruth warned. "They don't know you as well as they know us, Josh." She yawned and stretched out on the cushions.

"They do now," he chuckled, swiveling toward her. Then he lowered his camcorder and looked at his twin. "What's up, Ruthie? Are you flaking out this early?"

"It's been a long day," Ruth said.

PJ checked the time. "Whoops. Sorry, Ruth," she said. She stood up to go. "LG, BG, leave some seeds for Squirt. Let's wander home together, see if we can spot other owls?"

The gulls looked up, then eyed the leftover carrot cake longingly.

"Uh-uh." Ruth shook her head. "You know sugar isn't good for you!"

"C'mon, gulls," said PJ. She hugged Ruth and Josh and thanked everyone for the greatest bird rescue of all time.

"Hey, thank *you*, PJ," said Josh. "It's the first time my clips have hit TV!"

"Bye," said Ruth. "Josh, can you toss the ladder down for PJ?"

It started to drizzle as PJ walked home with the gulls wheeling above. They could hear loud guffaws through neighbors' open windows during the late-night TV news. They went past Mr. Splitzky's house but it was dark and silent. After that, BG and LG waved goodbye and said it was time to hit the coast to thank the Gull Gang. PJ gave them the bag with the rest of the fancy birdseed. Off they flew, the bag dangling from LG's webbed feet.

PJ hesitated at Mr. Splitzky's front gate. Should she check the barn? But she didn't want Blossom to start barking. Instead she placed two fingers in her mouth and gave a short, sharp whistle.

Nothing.

She whistled again.

Nothing.

She waited in the shadows. There was no sign of the owls, but something beautiful was happening. It wasn't just the bright moon, the gentle smell of rain in the air, and the dark sky. She rubbed her eyes to make sure she wasn't dreaming. A *moonbow*! Shimmering bands of

colored light arched over the space where LG and BG had just flown toward the cliffs, above Mrs. Patel's special waterfall! PJ stood on tiptoe and held her breath as though any noise or movement might disturb it.

In that moment, PJ felt the moonbow had appeared for her and the gulls, the night's special way of thanking them for the safe release of so many birds. She stood so still, her legs began to ache. She opened and closed her eyes several times, creating moonbow snapshots in her mind. Then she walked home slowly, went to her room, and sketched the beautiful moonbow over and over while it was fresh in her memory.

Later, her mom tapped on her door. She came into the room and asked, "PJ, did you see the news? A whole bunch of gulls attacked Tweety's. Everyone's talking about it. I never liked the man. He used to run those cruel puppy mills before switching to birds."

PJ closed her sketchbook. "Mom, it was like something out of a horror movie, wasn't it?"

Mrs. Picklelime was quiet for a while, then she said, "PJ, I'm leaving tomorrow, and—"

"So soon?" PJ cut in.

"The sooner I go, the sooner I'll be home."

PJ got up and hugged her mom for a long time.

"Don't you mean a lunar halo?" Mr. Picklelime asked over breakfast. "You know, a whitish circle that goes around the moon?"

"No, Dad, I mean a *moonbow*!" PJ said. She shaped a perfect arc with her hands. "It has all the same lovely colors as a rainbow. Only much softer."

"It's also known as a lunar rainbow," her mom cut in. "I've only seen photos of moonbows in Hawaii or southern Africa. They usually happen when bright moonlight hits rain or huge waterfalls. You're so lucky, PJ."

"Lucky?" Mr. Picklelime shrugged. "But I don't want her creeping around outside at night."

"*I* crept around gardens at night at PJ's age watching raccoons and possums," said Mrs. Picklelime.

"Things were different where you grew up," he said.

"Not really," Mrs. Picklelime said.

PJ could sense an argument brewing and quickly changed the subject. "I drew the moonbow. Look!" She produced her sketch pad and explained that she drew it over and over to get the shimmering colors exactly right.

"Art and animals. PJ, isn't it time you got serious?" her dad said.

PJ closed her sketchbook. They all sat in silence as he finished his scrambled eggs. Then he got up, mumbled something about needing to get to work early, and went out.

"It's OK, PJ," her mom said when Mr. Picklelime left the house. "This has nothing to do with your art and animals."

"I know." PJ finished her orange juice. "Did your parents get on your case when you went to watch raccoons at night?"

"They never found out," her mom admitted.

PJ and her mother smiled at one another.

PJ said nothing for a moment, then, "I saw your bags by the front door. You're leaving straight after breakfast?"

Her mom nodded. "I'm depending on you, PJ. I *love* the way you and Mrs. Patel planted herbs in the window boxes. Keep surprising me, honey. When I come home for the weekend, I'll bring twin tumbler bins so you can start composting. Come, let's water the plants together before I go."

☼

PJ invited Ruth and Joshua to join her in Mr. Splitzky's barn after school—with his permission, of course—so they could check on the owls and see which ones had returned home. Joshua came armed with his tiny camcorder. Blossom trotted along behind them up the path, tail wagging happily.

The four of them stood there in the dim interior of the honey-scented barn and gazed up at the familiar crisscross rafters and beams. Because Mr. Splitzky built both structures, the barn seemed like the grandparent of Ruth's tree house.

Suddenly some twigs floated down to the left of them from a dark corner high above.

"There!" shouted Joshua, aiming his camcorder.

"Shhh," whispered PJ.

Two familiarly pointed ears shot up from a nest where a beam joined the sloping wood interior of the roof.

"Oohoo?" PJ shouted. "It's us!"

The owl came swooping down to a lower beam, followed by two white-faced barn owls.

PJ, Ruth, and Joshua whooped and cheered. The owls bowed graciously.

"Oohoo, I am so happy to see you!" PJ said.

"The guys want to thank you and those wild gulls," said Oohoo. "Meet Monkey Face, to my left. And Tyto, to my right," she said, pointing a wing in each direction, like an actor introducing two white-masked friends.

"Heeeyyyy," chorused the twins. Joshua took a step back and raised his camcorder to catch the full effect of the trio above.

PJ said, "You don't need to thank us. I'll give the gulls your message. How did you find your way home last night?"

All three owls rolled their huge eyes. "Come on, PJ. Don't you know?" Oohoo said.

"Instinct?" PJ guessed.

"Hooo nooooo," said Oohoo. "How do you think birds fly across whole continents when the seasons change?"

"They follow landmarks?" Ruth asked.

"More than that. Birds have special eyes," Monkey Face explained. "Birds can see lines of energy in the air. Like you see roads."

"You see them in colors?" PJ asked.

"Some of us do," said Tyto.

"Cool!" PJ, Ruth, and Joshua chorused.

Talking about colors reminded PJ of what she had seen the night before. She told everyone about the beautiful moonbow and how she believed it was the sky's way of thanking them and the gulls for the SWAT-style rescue.

"I think you're right, PJ. Nothing goes unnoticed in nature, does it?" Ruth said. Then, looking at the owls, she asked, "Hey, guys, did *all* of you escape yesterday?"

"Yes, but . . ." Monkey Face looked at Oohoo sadly.

"My chicks haven't returned. I was hoping . . ." Big tears plopped down Oohoo's mottled feathers.

Tyto piped up. "They weren't at Tweety's. We're so sorry."

The two barn owls leaned forward. "There was a tiny chick, come to think of it," said Monkey Face. "Don't believe it was an owl. *Tiny*. It dropped behind." He closed his eyes and tried to remember.

"It went into a tree over there," said Tyto. She pointed a wing tip eastward. "Come on, friends. Tonight, let's spread out and hoot and *sssss* and screech and see if we can find it."

All of a sudden, the barn door banged open.

The owls immediately lifted off the beam and disappeared into their dark corner.

"It's OK, gang," Mr. Splitzky chuckled as he walked in. "This old barn is much happier with all of you here. It's *alive*. Even the bees are humming louder. That's good for my honey." He gestured toward the rows of jars lined up on either side of the doors. Then, cupping his hands around his mouth, he called out, "Hear me, owls, just take care of the mice!"

"Oh, they will," PJ reassured him.

"You kids are the greatest," said Mr. Splitzky. "Josh, keep up the good camera work." He winked. "Ruth, how many critters are you taking care of in the tree house these days?"

"Just Squirt the squirrel," she said.

"Not for long." PJ smiled.

"Well, I think I could do with a little break," Ruth admitted. "You can take care of the next bunch, PJ. I'm pooped. And I'm behind in math."

They all looked at her. It was unlike Ruth to worry about school.

"No problem," said PJ. Puzzled, she looked at one twin and then at the other.

"I'll help you catch up, Ruth," Joshua promised.

"Sounds like it's time you kids went home," Mr. Splitzky cut in cheerfully. "Help yourselves to some jars of honey for your folks on your way out. Come back and visit us whenever you like!"

Later that night the owls swooped out around town making every possible call they knew and eventually found the tiny chick, not an owl at all, but a baby black-and-white magpie, huddled, frightened and hungry, in the curve of a pecan tree branch. The three owls lifted him out carefully, named him Domino, and took him home with them, way up into the rafters above Mr. Splitzky's barn.

Right away, Oohoo took funny little black-and-white Domino under her wing. She decided to set up camp there with them all for a while since she didn't feel strong enough to find a tree nest on her own. She had become used to being indoors in Ruth's tree house. Anyway, setting up camp with others was a lot more fun than being alone. She even took the barn owls around the windows of the Chocolate Dream to show Evi Lenz they were back in town.

Ms. Lenz was so happy to see and hear them again at night, she made some special owl-shaped chocolates with peppermint eyes, ears, and little feet and displayed them in her window beside the lemon truffles.

With less to do in the tree house, PJ welcomed Mrs. Patel's help in the garden. Together they raked over the Picklelimes' veggie patch to plant rows of lettuce, spinach, beets, carrots, and radishes. PJ stapled lengths of twine along the ground to keep the lines beautifully straight. She planted beans and honeysuckle close to the fence. She also planted climbing jasmine against the trellis under her window. But she knew she would have to train it to grow up only one side so that she could skim down the other side at night.

"The art of creating a garden is to have a mix of plants and shrubs that flourish in different seasons, PJ," Mrs. Patel said after wheeling a barrow full of young flowering rosemary bushes over to the Picklelimes' to plant in bare and scruffy areas as ground cover. "Rosemary stays green and strong all year and grows beautifully in full sun. Snap some twigs for pretty displays on the kitchen table. It smells lovely. Or boil potatoes and sprinkle sprigs of rosemary over them with a little sea salt. *Delicious!*"

With PJ indoors and Mrs. Patel outdoors, the two tracked one another from window to window to plan new plants for the best views.

"I know what I want," PJ said when she ran down into the garden. "Pretty pink and red bushes and flowers to attract masses of butterflies and hummingbirds we can enjoy watching from all the windows."

"Good choice," said Mrs. Patel. "Oh, I've been meaning to talk to you about something, child."

The seriousness in her voice told PJ this had nothing to do with butterflies and pink bushes. "Yes, Mrs. Patel?" she said, shading her eyes from the sun.

"Helicopter Pete left all of a sudden. Someone said he was offered a job in Singapore, or was it São Paulo?" She paused. "Funny thing is this: Mr. Tweety the pet store owner left with him."

"*All right!*" PJ whooped.

"Of course their departure wouldn't have anything to do with you, or those birds escaping from Tweety's, would it, PJ?"

PJ grinned but said nothing.

"And you didn't know that Helicopter Pete was seen running for his life, surrounded by swarms of angry seagulls?"

PJ frowned, totally baffled. So Big Gull and Little Gull had organized this on their own? Way to go!

"Well, let's say our community lost some bad

apples." Mrs. Patel sighed. "But a little word of advice, here, PJ."

"Mrs. Patel?"

"Next time, if you and Ruth suspect something, talk to the police. Because we don't know what those two scoundrels will do next, do we, child?"

The thought hadn't even occurred to PJ. "At least Tweety's name is all over the Internet now."

"True. Still, don't get too reckless, PJ, will you?"

"I won't, Mrs. Patel," PJ said, and kept her fingers crossed behind her back.

ruth

While waiting for her mom to come home on the weekend, PJ felt a need to do something very practical with her dad. Something that wouldn't end in an argument. So she asked him to help her paint her room egg-yolk yellow.

"*Egg*-yolk yellow, PJ? Such a strong color?" he said, raising his eyebrows.

"Oh, Dad. It's *sooooo* my color this year!"

"Next year it'll be red?" He smiled.

PJ laughed. "We'll see," she said. Together they went to buy drop cloths, egg-yolk yellow paint, rollers, paint trays, and brushes. Ready to tackle the task together, PJ and her dad moved everything in her room into the center, draped it carefully, and layered the drop cloths on the floor.

Mr. Picklelime showed PJ how to pour paint into the trays, then spread it back and forth before rolling it on the walls, careful to avoid drips. He masked the windows and painted the rims an even darker shade of yellow, PJ's choice.

"Wouldn't you prefer white trim, PJ?" asked her dad.

"No way," PJ said, sweeping the roller up and down. She didn't want white trim or ledges, because they would show webbed bird footprints too clearly. But she didn't tell her dad that. "Dad, thanks," PJ said. "This'll be like living in a sunflower."

"Sounds nicer than living in egg yolk," he said.

Later, when everything was dry, they moved the furniture back and PJ reorganized all her pastel drawings in sequence on the corkboard opposite her bed. The yellow wall was the perfect backdrop to the array of drawings of birds, moons, gardens, the tree house, Ruth, and sunsets on display. It was getting quite crowded.

PJ lit some sandalwood incense, a gift from Mrs. Patel, to mask the paint smell, even though they were careful to buy a nontoxic variety. She was so excited about her new room, she hopped on her bike in her paint-spattered jeans and T-shirt, now covered in yellow, and cycled over to Ruth's house to tell her and to share the news about Pete and Tweety's departure. She also wanted to find out how Squirt was doing alone since the birds had found new homes.

Ruth's street was blocked by cars.

Puzzled, PJ dismounted and pushed her bike the rest of the way. People she didn't know or barely recognized were going in and out of the gate. Then she spotted Mr. Splitzky with Blossom on the sidewalk. He had tears in his eyes.

"Oh, PJ, I'm so glad to see you. We're all heartbroken about Ruth."

"Heartbroken? What's happened?" PJ asked.

"You haven't heard? Your parents didn't tell you?" Mr. Splitzky looked distressed.

"Heard what? Is Ruth sick?" PJ parked her bike at the curb.

Mr. Splitzky couldn't speak for a moment. He turned away and looked down, as though studying his feet. "PJ, I hate to be the person to share the news with you. There isn't an easy way of telling you. Your wonderful friend Ruth is no longer with us."

"You mean she left town?" PJ looked confused. "Was she kidnapped? Is that why there're so many cars here?"

Mr. Splitzky shook his head. "PJ, Ruth died earlier today."

"*Died?*" PJ's voice rose. "Mr. Splitzky, that's *sooooo* impossible. We were in your barn a few days ago talking about owls!"

"PJ, hold Blossom for a moment," he said.

PJ bobbed down and buried her face in Blossom's golden fur. *This isn't real*, she thought. Children didn't die just like that. Ruth wasn't even sick! "Did she have a bike accident? Did a car hit her? Did she fall out of the tree house?" she asked.

Mr. Splitzky shook his head. "They're still trying to figure out what happened," he explained. "One of those rare things, PJ. Hard to tell so early. Hard for any of us to understand. No advance warning. She felt this strong pain and died in the ambulance."

"There was nothing *wrong* with her, Mr. Splitzky. This can't be true!" More cars wove by, hunting for a parking space. Families got out, heads bowed. "Are you sure it wasn't her *great-grandmother* who died?"

"I'm so sorry, PJ, but no. Come, let's walk home together. This isn't the best time for you to see her family."

"But Squirt the squirrel's in the tree house at the back . . . ," PJ began, pointing toward the sprawling live oak branches she could see sticking out above the roof. "I need to go there."

"Tomorrow, PJ. Let Josh take care of things like that right now. They're all in shock."

PJ held both hands on Blossom. The dog's soft fur, rhythmic breathing, and warm body comforted her. Children didn't just die. Something was horribly wrong. After a moment, PJ lifted her hands off Blossom, reached for her bicycle, and followed Mr. Splitzky home. "I want to see Ruth," she said.

"That's not a good idea, PJ. Doctors are still examining her to find out exactly what went wrong. And then there's the Jewish ritual of wrapping the body, done by experts who are specially trained. Kind people will be very loving and careful when they touch her body. You can go with me to the funeral in a few days if you like."

Funeral? PJ blocked the word. She followed Mr. Splitzky and Blossom home in silence, too stunned to understand what was going on, and refusing to believe she wouldn't see Ruth ever again. She kept thinking about Ruth's gold-flecked gray eyes and the way she twirled her honey-blond pigtail to help her solve some problem. "Mr. Splitzky, what do you think happens when someone dies?"

"Ah, PJ," he explained, "I was raised in a Jewish household, like Ruth, and like Ms. Lenz. Traditionally we believe in the *here* and the *now*. I wasn't raised to believe in an afterlife. But talk to Mrs. Patel, PJ. She'll share her Hindu thoughts on reincarnation. Ask your art teacher, Mr. Santos, about Catholic beliefs. Talk to Mr. Kanafani about Islam. Ask Mrs. Martins about Protestant beliefs. Go and talk to Ms. Naguri about Zen Buddhism. Then you can make up your own mind."

"How will this help me?" PJ asked.

"Just listen," said Mr. Splitzky. He placed a comforting arm around PJ's shoulders. "Keep Ruth in your mind and heart. You will soon hear something to help you make sense of this unhappy day."

She stood by the gate and watched Mr. Splitzky go, followed by Blossom swishing her tail. PJ longed to talk to her mother or to Mrs. Patel. But first she needed to go off alone. She began to feel a heaviness close around her heart, so she climbed back on the seat of her bike and pedaled toward the cliffs.

The loss made her think about Lemon Pie and how much she missed him, how much she would miss Ruth. If

she felt this way, how must Josh be feeling? And Ruth's parents? Mr. Splitzky said it was too soon to see them, but if all those other people could, why couldn't she?

The wind was brisk. It whipped her cheeks and tugged her curls. She felt the sting of salt spray. A couple frolicked with dogs on the beach below, but PJ preferred to stay up on the cliffside. She didn't want to risk bumping into anyone she knew. Gulls tumbled about in the strong wind, but she didn't recognize any of them. BG and LG were nowhere in sight.

She thought about Ruth's advice, about learning to let go, giving animals and friends the strength to move on, to be free, to find their own space.

But how could you let go before you understood what it was that you were letting go? It was impossible for PJ to imagine she would never see Ruth again. PJ longed to talk to Joshua. She would call him soon, whether Mr. Splitzky said it was a good idea or not.

The wind got colder and fiercer. It flattened sea oats to the sandy crest of the cliff. PJ shivered. She wished she had one of her heavy fleece hoodies with her. She jumped on her bike again and headed home.

Her mom's car was in the driveway. Had she come home early because of Ruth's death?

PJ locked her bicycle and went in slowly, wondering why she felt so numb. Her mother was on the phone in the front room, surrounded by books.

Mrs. Picklelime studied her daughter's face anxiously. She ended her call and reached out for PJ.

PJ hugged her and then pulled away. "It's not right."

"Honey, I lost my best friend at your age. I know how it feels."

PJ shook her head. "You can't know how I feel, Mom."

Mr. Picklelime poked his head around the door and said, "Sorry, sorry to hear about Ruth." When they didn't react, he asked, "Was she taking any sort of drugs? Kids do these days. If she was, I need to know if she gave you anything, PJ."

"Dad, how can you talk to me like that?"

Mrs. Picklelime held up her hands. "Philip, I'll take care of this. Why not give us a little space?"

When he left, PJ said, "Dad is so wrong. *So* wrong! You know that, don't you?"

"Course I do. Don't take any notice, PJ. He's over-anxious about you. That's all." She paused. "Mr. Splitzky called me, so I came home immediately. PJ, it's hard to find a way to explain such a tragedy. All you can do is keep a vivid picture of Ruth in your wonderful imagination and act on everything she taught you. This takes time, I know."

"Is that what you did after you lost your best friend?"

"I curled up with Peppy, our dog, in his kennel so no one could find me. My parents couldn't deal with it, so nothing was discussed. I worked things out on my own. That wasn't the best way. I shut down inside."

PJ listened. She understood a little of what her mom was saying about finding comfort in Peppy, because of the comfort she felt earlier while hugging Blossom. Now she realized why her mom kept a goofy picture of floppy-eared Peppy on display, even though the dog had died years and years ago.

Her mom cut into her thoughts. "PJ, it helps to keep doing really regular things at such times. Keep active. Look, why don't we set up the tumbler compost bins I brought home?"

When PJ didn't respond, she said, "I saw your wonderful yellow room." She smiled. "Looks like half the paint ended up on your jeans."

"Yes, well." PJ paused. Who cared about compost or paint-splattered jeans at such a time? "Mom, I need to go out again for a while, is that OK?" PJ asked, backing out of the room. Without waiting for her mother to reply, she left the house, knowing her parents would start to fight. This was one day she did not want to wait around to hear it.

She went straight to Mrs. Patel, who took her in her arms and held her for a long time without talking. "Come, child. Let's go in the kitchen. I just made some jasmine tea," she said. "I knew I'd see you today."

Mrs. Patel lifted a tea cozy shaped like a large ladybug off a round earthenware pot and poured them each a lightly scented cup. PJ watched the steam rise. She blew gently on the brew to cool it before taking her first sips. Mrs. Patel spooned in some sweet honey from Mr. Splitzky's bees.

PJ said, "Why is it I can sit with you in silence and you know exactly how I am feeling, Mrs. Patel?"

Mrs. Patel chuckled. "I listen to your silence, PJ. It's not that difficult. I have some news for you, child. I was with Ruth's parents today. They would like you to have the tree house."

"What about Joshua?" PJ asked in surprise.

Mrs. Patel shook her head. "He doesn't have that same passion for animals. But his parents know you do. Can you handle the tree house alone, PJ?"

PJ didn't answer right away. "I'm scared, Mrs. Patel."

"Scared of what, child? Of the tree house?"

"No, I love the tree house. I'm scared of not knowing where Ruth has gone."

"Ah, dear PJ, I understand that fear. It's important to put something in its place. Be a friend to Josh. Ruth would want that, you know." Mrs. Patel paused. "Also," she went on, "taking care of Ruth's animals, or any injured animal, will always keep you very close to her memory."

PJ thought about this. It didn't seem right for someone as good as Ruth to disappear just like that. Branches scraped against the roof above in a gust of wind. PJ got up to look outside. She wished her family's garden would hurry up and become as comfortingly lush as Mrs. Patel's. "Mr. Splitzky said I should ask you about reincarnation," she said.

Mrs. Patel laughed softly. "PJ, Ruth gave so much of herself. To her tree-house animals. To her friends, like you. To Josh. To her parents. Yes, she left us too soon and our hearts are breaking. We can't explain everything. She was a wonderful role model. Reincarnation? Will she return to our earth in another body? I believe we all keep returning to earth to evolve, become wiser, and complete unfinished business. Sometimes, we are linked once again—but in different ways—to our circle of friends and family from a previous life."

PJ turned from the window. "Does that mean I'll see her again?"

"Not in the same way or form, PJ. We don't know when Ruth might return. Or where. I do not expect you or anyone else to share my philosophy. Don't think too hard. Just keep her alive here," she said, tapping PJ's chest, "by continuing to do the work she loved."

"You believe that?" PJ asked.

"I do with all my heart. Come, child, let's finish our tea."

☀

Very early the next morning, PJ opened a window to see a familiar figure hunched up in a hoodie at her front gate. He held a canvas shopping bag that had something bulky, and something live, jumping up and down inside.

"*Josh?* Is that you?" PJ called out.

He waited for her to join him in the garden.

"Josh, I've been wanting to see you." PJ ran toward him.

He shook his head. "It's a nightmare, PJ. I can't feel anything. I can't even cry. Take Squirt and hide him," he said, and handed her the canvas bag. "Don't tell anyone. Those moron doctors are trying to say Ruth must have caught bird flu or rabies or something weird from the animals. If you and I aren't sick, how can they say that? I told my parents the birds and Squirt left already. Oh, I'm also giving you Ruth's soccer ball. I found him spread-eagled over it."

PJ took the bag carefully and held it close to her chest to calm Squirt. "They'd kill Squirt, wouldn't they?"

Josh nodded and dug his hands in his pockets. "Ruth wouldn't want that."

"Of course not."

They stood in silence for a moment. Then PJ said, "I heard your parents want me to have the tree house."

"It's my decision," Josh said tightly. "I can't bear to look at it knowing Ruth isn't there. She'd want you to have it, PJ."

"OK, but why not keep the tree house for a little while in case you change your mind?" PJ suggested.

"I won't change my mind," he said, and placed his hand over hers. "I better go home now. Thanks for taking care of Squirt."

"Anytime," she replied.

Joshua withdrew his hand slowly and turned away. PJ watched him walk to the corner. All the spring had gone out of his step. She looked from left to right, thankful no one had seen the exchange of the wriggling canvas bag. Now she had to navigate Squirt by her parents and into her room.

"Squirt, chill, OK?" she said, peeking into the bag when he started his usual *brrrkbrrrkbrrrking*. "I'm taking you home with me."

Mrs. Picklelime met her at the front door. "Who was that in the garden, PJ?"

"Joshua. He gave me Ruth's soccer ball," PJ said, crossing her arms protectively over the bag to keep Squirt quiet.

"How thoughtful of him," her mom said. She raised one eyebrow at the bag.

PJ turned to go up to her room.

"I'll be working down here if you need me, honey."

"OK, Mom, thanks," said PJ, climbing the stairs two at a time. She closed her door, headed straight for the freshly painted window seat, and opened the canvas bag. Squirt jumped out. His spiky gray fur looked as though someone had plugged his tail into an electric outlet.

PJ bounced the soccer ball a few times, hugged it tightly, and placed it beside the squirrel. He nudged it with his nose. She then went for the box she had once used for Messenger Gull's layover. It was still lined with an old red fleecy tartan shirt. Squirt jumped in. He lay there, looking up at PJ with sad eyes. His tail hung over the edge of the box, motionless.

PJ went over to her corkboard and studied the sketches she had done of Ruth recently. There was Ruth on her bicycle, pigtail flying in the wind. There was Ruth with Squirt dangling off her shoulder. PJ reached for her sketch pad to draw all of them in Mr. Splitzky's barn with the owls while the image was still fresh in her mind. Somehow, she couldn't seem to mix the right colors together. She couldn't even draw the outlines. She tried several times but nothing seemed to work. Finally she just closed the pad and sat on the window seat, with one hand on Squirt and the other on the soccer ball.

☀

Joshua called later to say the doctors had dismissed all suspicions of rabies or bird flu or any other animal-carried disease. "Some weird virus hit her," he explained in tears. "Ruth could have picked it up anywhere. Hit her like a meteorite, *bam!* She wasn't even *sick!*"

"But she seemed very tired all of a sudden, don't you remember?"

There was silence on the phone. "Hey, you're right, PJ," he said after a while. "I just thought all the excitement was too much."

"What about you, Josh?"

"Physically? Doctors gave me the all clear. What do they know? PJ, I'm feeling so empty. I want to rewind our lives like a movie. I keep thinking about things I wish I'd said."

PJ heard his voice break before he cut the call.

☀

A few days later, PJ, flanked by her parents, Mrs. Patel, Mr. Splitzky, Blossom, Ms. Lenz, and a huge tree full of birds and squirrels, attended Ruth's graveside funeral, along with scores of her friends and neighbors. Everyone sang, and the birds lifted the sky with their lovely chorus of voices.

One by one, Ruth's friends got up to talk about their best memories. PJ spoke about always seeing Ruth

cycling around the streets, hands off her handlebars, pigtail flying.

After Ruth's coffin was lowered into the ground, they
all lined up to scatter earth on their friend in a silent tribute. According to Jewish custom, they used the reverse
side of the spade, a simple, symbolic way of showing how
sad and difficult it was to say goodbye.

Big drops fell out of the sky. Everyone looked up,
thinking it had started to rain. But it was actually tears
from all the birds lined up on the branches of the leafy
oak tree.

pj's Search

Before Mr. Splitzky could dismantle the tree house and haul it over to the Picklelimes' garden, PJ did exactly what he had advised. When her mom left again, she went from neighbor to neighbor to hear their thoughts on what happened to someone—especially a child—after death.

Tall, thin Mr. Kanafani placed two little stools under his favorite orange tree because it was full of blossoms and the air was heavily scented in just that spot. He crossed his long legs in front of him like a pair of scissors.

"PJ," he began, staring into the distance, "yes, our sacred book the Koran talks a lot about *al-Akhirah*, the afterlife. Yes, some higher being judges us according to our good deeds and our bad deeds. But then what? I don't know. For me, Ruth was all about good deeds. Maybe that is all you need to know." He reached up and picked some orange blossoms. He held them in the palm of his right hand and stroked them gently, then inhaled the lovely scent. "Cup your hands for me," he said. He dropped soft petals into her upturned palms.

PJ buried her nostrils in the petals.

"You see, PJ," he said, "like Mrs. Patel, I let nature's cycles teach me all the mysteries I need to know. I grew my lovely orange trees from the seeds I brought with me from my hometown of Jericho. Every year my trees give me canopies of blossoms richer than the previous year. Then blossoms drop off and fruit begins to bud. Every year they give me more and more oranges, sweeter than the last year. We eat what we can. We boil peels in sugar for candies. We make marmalade and rich syrup for winter months." Mr. Kanafani touched the trunk lovingly. "Wait here. I have some tiny trees growing in pots. I would like you to have them. Plant them somewhere special in Ruth's memory." Mr. Kanafani rose, went into his house, and returned with two leafy little trees in clay pots and gave them to her.

PJ took the pots onto her lap and hugged them. "Mrs.

Patel is teaching me all her gardening secrets, Mr. Kanafani," she said. "I'll plant these in a special place. One day my garden will smell as lovely as yours and hers."

"You can enjoy those fragrances all year." He smiled. "We also place the peels on our wood-burning stoves in winter so our *entire* house is scented like an orange grove!"

While she listened to his every word, PJ became almost dizzy with the scent of the blossoms overhead.

"When branches fall in the winds," Mr. Kanafani explained, "we burn them and mix the ashes in our compost with leaves. When that breaks down into soil with scraps and peels from the kitchen, we dig it into the earth around the orange trees. So everything moves around and around in a cycle."

"That's so beautiful, Mr. Kanafani."

"That's my personal belief, dear PJ. It goes beyond anything I can read in the Koran about the afterlife. It's my link to the past and something I give to my children."

"Ruth didn't have orange trees," PJ said. "But she loved her live oaks and pecan trees."

"Then honor her, by taking some acorns and pecans from her garden in the fall. Plant some in your garden along with orange and lemon trees. Plant some in pots for the winter. Watch them grow. Add the shells to your own compost. Feed pecans to the birds and squirrels that loved her. This way, you keep her breath alive."

"Not just by taking care of her tree house?"

Mr. Kanafani shook his head. "Ruth was a special girl. Honor her every way you can. And accept."

"Accept?"

"By accepting her death you will find inner peace."

PJ went home and planted the little orange trees within view of the kitchen window. She dug some of Mrs. Patel's fresh compost into the soil, left a moat around the base of each tree, and watered them thoroughly. Then she took a pot of kitchen scraps and strips of newspaper out to her new composter and tumbled it around. The bin spun so fast PJ nearly flew off her feet.

Later, PJ went to see Ms. Kyoko Naguri from Nagasaki. She hadn't spoken to her since the day of the funeral. They sat together on a wooden bench next to a lily pond filled with koi fish that flopped about as if to show off their vivid colors and splotchy bodies.

PJ smiled at them. "Ms. Naguri, they look as though someone started to paint them and then couldn't finish."

Ms. Naguri threw back her head and clapped her hands. "Oh, PJ, I love your imagination! Follow me." She rose from the bench and led PJ across a curvy line of stepping stones to the other side of the pond. "Pause a little on each stone, PJ. Now, look down!"

Sure enough, the colorful koi came clustering around their feet. The fish flapped and flopped about in the deep green water and circled around the stepping stones. They were looking for treats, which PJ and Ms. Naguri gave them, encouraging yet more fish to jet across from the other side of the pond.

Ms. Naguri's short black hair swung around her friendly face and twinkling eyes like curtains blown by the wind. As she and PJ jumped from one stone to the next, she listened to what PJ told her about her time under the orange tree with Mr. Kanafani.

Ms. Naguri nodded wisely when PJ repeated Mr. Kanafani's thoughts on cycles. Her own Zen Buddhist belief in cycles of birth, death, and rebirth in nature helped her make sense of a chaotic and often unhappy world. "We also learn to make sense out of nonsense, and nonsense out of sense. It keeps us balanced," she added.

"I like that," said PJ.

"PJ, remember everything about Ruth that made you

laugh. Her jokes. Her funny pigtail. This is how she would want us all to remember her. Not to mourn and walk around with long faces!"

When Ms. Naguri and PJ reached the other side of the pond, they sat together on a bench made out of logs. PJ tossed the koi the last of the treats and watched them swim away. The day had become warm and balmy, a sign that spring was easing into summer.

"What does 'Zen' mean, Ms. Naguri?" PJ asked.

"Very simple. It means 'meditation.'"

"Is that what people mean when they say something is very 'Zen'? It makes them feel they are meditating?"

"Hmmm, more than that, PJ. It means many things. Focus. Awareness. Your ability to see the essence and purpose of something. For example"—Ms. Naguri pointed at the wavy line of round stones they had just used to cross the pond—"those stones are very Zen, because you need to focus on each step to keep your balance and to be mindful as you cross the water. In that way, you are more observant. So were the koi. They came swimming to greet us. They wouldn't have done that had we rushed across like folks running for a train."

PJ pondered this for a few moments as she watched

dragonflies skim across the water. "How do *you* meditate, Ms. Naguri?"

"I sit in this same spot every morning and meditate, PJ. I let my mind float with the sounds. Listen!" Water trickled over stones in a shallow part of the pond close to their feet. "When it rains," Ms. Naguri went on, "I love to watch *that*." She pointed at a flutelike bamboo fountain that tilted down with the weight of water, and then, when the water flowed out, tilted up with a snap to capture yet more water.

"Did you make that? And your bamboo wind chimes?" PJ nodded at the chimes hanging close by. They were quiet because the air was still.

"Oh yes." Ms. Naguri smiled. "I love to carve bamboo. I just finished a new rain fountain in my studio. It's a bit bigger than mine. Would you like to have it for your garden, PJ?"

"Are you sure?" PJ asked. "Will it make *plink-plink* noises when it rains? Like a tiny orchestra?"

"More than that," said Ms. Naguri. "You will hear different sounds in a light rain compared with a heavy rain."

PJ knew about the different noises rain made as it rushed through gutters and downspouts into their barrels at home. She'd place the fountain under her bedroom window so she could hear it at night. She also knew her bird buddies would enjoy drinking from it.

Then she had an idea. "Ms. Naguri, could you make bamboo wind chimes to hang on Ruth's live oak after Mr. Splitzky brings me her tree house?" she asked. "So Josh and her parents can fill that space with music?"

"That's a lovely idea!" Ms. Naguri said. "Then the whole block will think of Ruth each time breezes visit us." She smiled, then added, "PJ, I know you love that tree house. But don't hide in it too much. Keep finding new joy in your own garden and home."

☀

"PJ, why can't you have a dog or a cat like other kids your age?" Mr. Picklelime complained when he met her later, carrying her new rain fountain through the front gate. "I'm tired of those scruffy seagulls pooping on the lawn. Aren't they supposed to poop on the beach?"

"Oh, come on, Dad, they're just fertilizing the grass," said PJ. "They aren't hurting anyone."

"Well, it's interesting the way they seem to follow you

home. The instant I come into the garden they make awful noises and fly off."

"Maybe if you sat outside quietly they wouldn't fly off?"

He didn't reply but stared at the bamboo fountain in her hands. "What's that contraption?"

PJ explained how it worked and then asked him to help her find a suitable spot for it under her bedroom window.

He pointed up at a corner in the rain collection gutter on the roof, close to a downspout. "When it rains heavily there's always overspill in this area, PJ, so it's perfect for your fountain just below. You can direct the spout onto whatever you are trying to grow up this trellis."

"Jasmine," she told him, hoping he wouldn't ask why it was planted off center. She had to leave a space so she could scale down the trellis from her bedroom window.

Mr. Picklelime didn't seem to notice. He scouted around, gathering rocks to secure the base of the fountain. "There," he said, then, with a glance at the sky, added, "Now all we need is rain."

"Dad, *thanks*," said PJ. She went to get the watering can to try out the new fountain and also drizzle water over her new plants and herbs, all of which were beginning to grow nicely. Later, she joined her dad in the kitchen.

"Hungry? I think Mom left something here for us," he said, opening the freezer door. "Lasagna? Ravioli?"

"No thanks, it's too much," said PJ. "I think I just want yogurt and fruit, Dad."

"That's all I feel like, too."

Together they chopped apples, peaches, and bananas into a big bowl and stirred in a pot of strawberry yogurt with some crushed pecans from their past fall crop. PJ made tea from a fresh mint plant that Mrs. Patel had given her.

They ate in silence until Mr. Picklelime said, "Everyone's talking about Ruth. It's a tragedy when a child dies. Parents never get over it. I'm so sorry."

"It's OK, Dad. I'm working through this. It helps to know her tree house will be here soon."

"Wouldn't it be better for you to visit your other school friends?" he said as he stirred honey into his mint tea. "It doesn't seem right somehow. You really want to spend time in a dead friend's tree house?"

PJ shrugged. "Ruth isn't a 'dead' friend, Dad. She's someone I'll always remember."

Mr. Picklelime sighed and said, "Tree house or no tree house, PJ, don't neglect school and your duties around here. I don't want to come home and find cockroaches running all over a sink full of dirty dishes."

"You won't, Dad. I promise."

"Thanks, PJ." He finished his fruit, and chewing on the spring of mint from his tea, he left her alone.

After he was gone, PJ took the fruit peels and bits out to the compost. Luckily, none of her bird buddies had flown in. She didn't want them to confront her dad. Reassured that the coast was clear, she went to her room to complete an essay for class, on neighbors. She wrote about everything she had seen that day, Mr. Kanafani's lovely orange blossoms, Ms. Naguri's pond with the koi, dragonflies, wavy line of stepping stones, bamboo fountain, and wind chimes.

She reached for her sketch pad and pastels to try to capture those images on paper. But somehow she still couldn't seem to get the right mix of colors or forms. It was as though her hand just froze. She hadn't been able to add any new sketches to the corkboard since Ruth's death. Was this "freezing" something everyone experienced after losing a friend? How long would it last?

Squirt interrupted her thoughts by flying from a branch to the window ledge and onto her shoulder. He draped himself around her neck in the same way he used to drape himself around Ruth. Except he lay there quietly, very different from his usual chattering and twitching about.

PJ stroked his fur until he drifted off. She eased him from her shoulder and into his box beside her bed. Then she looked through the reading assignment Mr. Flax had given them to prepare for tomorrow's class. They were going down to the beach to help coastal and wildlife crews clean up and document debris, and plant grasses on the dunes to replace those damaged by the oil spill. Feeling sleepy, she climbed under the covers and spent a restless night swimming across the ocean in a dream with koi fish the size of dolphins.

PJ felt some of her sadness lift as she ran around on the beach in a blustery wind with her botany class. Her mom was right. It was important to throw herself into regular activities. She was far from the area where her gull friends normally hung out, but even so, she found herself looking up each time she heard a familiar *caw-caw-caw*.

Decked out in protective gloves and boots, PJ and her classmates helped the crews fill garbage bins with junk littering the beach, like broken sandals and plastic buckets, soda and beer cans. They also documented the debris that washed up on shore from boats, wrecks, storms, and distant countries, like ships' timbers, bottles, anchors, entire palm trees, and even an old trunk filled with sand. They found dead birds trapped in huge clumps of seaweed, some still matted with oil. Any industrial waste they red-flagged for the coastal crews to document, remove, and trace back to points of origin to file complaints.

"Why do we need to help restore the dunes after storms and oil spills?" Mr. Flax asked when the class had completed their share of cleanup and gathered around him in a circle.

"Dunes protect the beach?" someone said.

"How?" Mr. Flax asked.

"They hold the sand together and prevent it from blowing away."

"How?" Mr. Flax asked again.

"Grasses and plants help to bind the dunes," said PJ. "Then birds can nest in them. It's a whole other ecosystem."

"Exactly," said Mr. Flax. Next to him was a trolley load of sea oats, beach grass, morning glory vines, and goldenrod he had wheeled onto the dunes. He handed out spades and trowels and told the class where and how to start planting to replace grasses that had been destroyed by the oil spill.

"Their roots go way, way down," he said, "and they also help to filter out pollutants left by oil and anything else—which is why you must never pull up or destroy sea oats or dune grasses. Don't feel tempted to pick the pink or yellow or purple flowers you see growing across the dunes on vines. Enjoy them, photograph them, but leave them alone."

After the digging and planting activities, the class loaded their spades and trowels onto the trolley and trundled back to the school bus. Their cheeks were windblown to a bright cherry red. Salt spray made their hair, especially PJ's, look like explosions.

When they returned to school, PJ asked Mr. Flax if she could have a few moments alone with him during the lunch break.

"Of course, PJ."

"Mr. Flax, do plants have souls?" she asked. "Is that why seeds from a dead plant can create new flowers?"

He smiled down at her. "What do you think, PJ?"

"I know seeds have a special energy that makes them grow. People have different energies, but after they die they don't sprout little people like seeds sprout little flowers. So where does their soul energy go?"

Mr. Flax said, "Hmmm." He knew why PJ was asking

these questions. "PJ, in my church we talk about the soul going toward light, toward God. The soul comes from God, and returns to God, the highest and purest form of energy."

"Doesn't God need plants?"

"He gives us the gift of plants for beauty, and to nourish us. We best serve God when we honor and respect people, plants, and *all* forms of life," Mr. Flax said.

"That's God's work on earth?"

"A big part of God's work, yes, PJ. Does that help?"

"It makes me *think*. Do you know Mr. Splitzky, the 'bearded beekeeper'? And Blossom, his dog? He said I should talk to a lot of people, ask a lot of questions about life and death."

Mr. Flax nodded. Everyone knew Mr. Splitzky and Blossom. "Mr. Splitzky's honeybees actually stop caterpillars from eating plants in your neighborhood. Caterpillars don't like the vibration *bzzz-bzzzing* the air, so they move away!"

"He never told us that," said PJ. "That's great news for our gardens!"

"It sure is. He's a good man and he's given you good advice," said Mr. Flax, gathering up his books. "Keep on asking questions, PJ. You will get many different answers.

Don't be confused. Let different questions and answers play around in your thoughts like different tunes. You know how that goes? Until a favorite tune keeps on playing over and over in your mind?" Pausing to pick up his laptop, he smiled at her. "I'll let you in on a little secret. Your art teacher, Mr. Santos, and I are planning an exciting project together for the end of the semester. I know you're quite the artist. You'll love it!"

"What's the project?"

"Can't tell you now."

PJ turned away. "Mr. Flax, I haven't been able to draw anything since Ruth died."

Mr. Flax said, "Look at me, PJ. Grief hits all of us in different ways. Some feel sad. Others feel angry. Some kids shut down so they don't feel anything at all. Be patient with yourself. Your art is just taking a rest."

"I hope so."

"I know so. That's another reason why you should go talk to Mr. Santos."

CHAPTER 12

the gull gang

Pablo dos Santos y Sanchez did a swift U-turn on his racing bike and pedaled after PJ when he spotted her cycling toward a jagged split in the cliffside not far from Mrs. Patel's waterfall. Below, the ocean was a choppy, restless gray, flecked with foam.

"Whoa!" he said. "You are cycling like the wind these days, PJ! Mr. Splitzky and Mr. Flax said you wanted to see me. Come—let's drop our bikes over there by that big boulder and talk a little!"

Mr. Santos was not only PJ's art teacher but a wonderful sculptor who created beautiful objects and fountains in stone for meditation gardens and to catch the eye of people who walked into office buildings and universities. He ordered his stone from surrounding quarries.

"I add shape to what I see in nature," he told PJ. "Nature does eighty percent of the work. See this?" Mr. Santos sat down in a bowl-like niche on the boulder, which was deeply scalloped by centuries of wind and water. He tapped the rock as PJ sat down beside him. "Look at all these contours and funny shapes," he said. "Look how tiny sea creatures got trapped here and here." He pointed out some shellfish fossils. "See where little plants and flowers sprouted out of a few grains of dust blown here by the wind. *Milagro!* A miracle!"

"Mr. Santos, you sound like Mr. Flax. He also taught us how to look for tiny plants growing out of rocks and roofs." Feeling the warmth of the rock through her hands, PJ asked, "How would you sculpt this rock if nature has done most of the work?"

Mr. Santos got up and circled it thoughtfully. Every now and then, he bobbed down to examine some crevice or to run his long fingers over a jagged edge. "Perfect," he said. "I'd leave the areas that nature has claimed exactly as you see them here. Then, ah, then I would use this lovely bowl shape on the top for a special fountain. Sand it carefully to smooth out the roughness so you can see the grain in the stone. Look at all these lovely patterns. Look at the seams of pink quartz, PJ . . . PJ? Hello? Anyone at home?"

PJ didn't respond and Mr. Santos just smiled and said, "Eh!"

Clouds raced across a gray sky that matched the color of the ocean. The waves seemed choppier than usual. Everything seemed to be churning, including PJ's own emotions. She appreciated Mr. Santos's intensity, but her mind was far away. "My neighbors have been sharing all their thoughts with me about what happens after death. What's your belief?"

"Well, I'm an artist, PJ, so that's what I will share," he said. "Not some traditional Catholic belief!"

"That's OK," said PJ. "I hate it when people talk to me like a baby and say Ruth is 'in a better place' or 'up there' somewhere," she said, gesturing toward the sky. "Up where?"

Mr. Santos folded his hands. "When I was a schoolboy of your age in Spain," he said, "my teachers were monks who drummed dramatic ideas in our head about mortal sin and heaven and hell, and a sort of midway place called purgatory, where you went if you weren't bad enough for hell or good enough for heaven. *Pfffft!*" he said with a flick of a hand. "By the time I went to art school, I shed all that like a skin. I began to see life and especially art as one big school. Training us to learn. To be sensitive. Kind. To listen. To observe. Yes, to do crazy things sometimes and fall down." He laughed in his musical way. "We also learn from one another—as you learned from Ruth. You are growing through everything she taught you. So, in many ways, she is still among us. Only her *physical* form is not."

"It's still hard, Mr. Santos."

"I know, PJ. Ask yourself this. What would your life be like if you had not met Ruth?"

PJ thought for a moment. "I wouldn't have learned so much or have all these cool animal and bird friends!"

"Ah. So her work with you was complete? You learn fast. Now, does it help you to think of her in some invisible form somewhere, teaching others?"

PJ sighed. "What you are saying is that I need to *share* her with the universe, right?"

"You could think of it that way, why not?" Mr. Santos said.

"I'll try, Mr. Santos," she said, close to tears. "I don't understand why I can't seem to draw anything at the moment. I can't even draw Ruth."

"Don't worry, PJ. Don't force yourself. Wait until things happen spontaneously. Just spend these days doing things that come easily. Cycle, garden, work extra hard at school. Ah, go to the library and enjoy the most beautiful art books."

That seemed like a good idea to PJ and was also an excuse to talk to the librarian, Mrs. Martins.

Mr. Santos leaned down and let a handful of sand trickle through his fingers. "Look, PJ, nothing is separate from us," he said. "We are all made up of tiny particles moving at different speeds and in different shapes and forms. Even this sand has minerals in it that we also have in our bodies."

"Is that art? Or science?" PJ asked.

"Oh, PJ, an artist would say art. A scientist would say science. What do you think?"

"Is there really a difference?"

"Is ice cream art or science?"

"Both!" PJ smiled.

"Good! Let's jump on our bikes to see if we agree on that over vanilla cones swirled with peanut butter, caramel, and crushed nuts. I'll tell you about the art show Mr. Flax and I are planning for the end of the semester. We're looking for some hot creativity from you!"

"PJ, is that you, my girl?" Mrs. Martins came *tap-tap-tap*ping down her ladder after replacing books on the top shelf in the library's science section.

PJ waited below, arms laden with art books. "Hi, Mrs. Martins. Do you have ten minutes for me?"

"Come into my little den, PJ." Mrs. Martins led the way through the stacks and between tables of readers by the bay windows to an office behind the front desk. She ruffled PJ's hair and said, "Doesn't take long for it to grrrrrow wild again, hey, PJ? When the sea air's heavy and damp like today, we say bushy hair like ours is 'going home to Africa,' you know?"

PJ liked that idea and thought about the way her curls helped mop up oil on the waves. Perhaps her hair floated all the way to Africa, along with Lemon Pie? It was nice to hear Mrs. Martins's clipped accent and rolled *rrrrr's* because they reminded her of Messenger Gull's b-mail visit.

She perched herself on a tall stool opposite Mrs. Martins and said, "I'm asking all my neighbors to help me understand life and death."

Mrs. Martins's eyebrows shot up. "And you're trying

to find answers in art books?" she said. "Fire away, PJ. Ask anything you like."

"Mr. Splitzky said you were a Protestant."

Mrs. Martins hooted with laughter. "Nay, my girl. I can't be pinned down in a box like that. Remember I grrrrrew up in an area of Cape Town where we had Muslim spice sellers on one side of the street, Indian textile merchants on the other side, and a Jewish furniture shop on the corner. One little Catholic church squeezed in here, and a Methodist church squeezed in there. One family worshiped on Friday, another on Saturday, and others on Sunday. So I thought, God is far too overworked. When our minister started on about repenting sins and looking for grace through Christ for everlasting life, I thought, wait. It's action that counts. Not words."

PJ leaned forward. "How old were you, Mrs. Martins?"

"A few years older than you, my girl. But remember I grew up under a terrrrrible past political system that was hell on earth. I didn't need some minister to tell me about an abstract hell. We lived it, hey? I thought to myself, I have responsibility for my own soul in the same way I have responsibility for my body. Exercise, eat the rrrrright foods, no cigarettes or booze. In the same way, feed and exercise the soul. Think. Change political darkness to light in the community. Spread goodness. Swim, walk in the mountains. Feel God's abundance. Be aware, hey?"

"You make it sound so simple, Mrs. Martins," said PJ. She remembered Lemon Pie's b-mail about spreading seeds from the sacred fig tree that started to bear fruit again when the politics of South Africa changed.

"It *is* simple, PJ. Create a special energy around yourself to give others joy, hope. God supplies the raw material. It's up to us what we do with it."

"Ruth did a lot."

"That's it! Otherwise you wouldn't be rrrrrunning around asking all these questions, my girl."

꩜

That evening, PJ sat on her window seat and replayed everything she had learned that day, the beach activities, and all the thoughts she had shared with Mr. Flax, Mr. Santos, and Mrs. Martins. Breezes brought the smell of the ocean right into her room. She could hear the comforting and familiar sound of Mrs. Patel's melodic metal chimes across the road. The moon was crystal clear, like a circle of pure ice in the sky, forming a perfect triangle with two brilliant stars. The owls were silent tonight, or perhaps it was too early? Her dad was watching TV downstairs, but all she could hear was a faint murmur.

A feeling of peace came over her for the first time in days. Her mind wasn't racing like a bicycle going downhill without brakes anymore, but she knew this was also probably because she felt weary in a nice way. Outside, the rosebush was just a dark shape against the fence. She could also see the outlines of the little orange trees and the small pink and red flowering bushes she had planted within view of her windows to attract bees, butterflies, and hummingbirds.

PJ especially loved the idea that Mr. Splitzky's bees might visit her flowers and keep caterpillars away. One day she would taste his honey and know that some of that nectar came from her garden.

The breezes shifted outside. Now she could hear the gentle hollow sounds of Ms. Naguri's bamboo chimes. They mingled beautifully with Mrs. Patel's metal chimes. What could she choose for one of her trees to harmonize with their music? Bells, perhaps?

That reminded her of Ms. Lenz and her cluster of bell-like copper curls with their sweet ring only PJ could hear. Maybe that was what composers could hear, noises and rhythms in people and nature that were silent to everyone else? Wasn't that the sort of thing Mrs. Martins was describing about creating something out of God's raw material?

Could composers hear the moon? People were always singing to or about the moon. So if the moon absorbed all those songs and those lovely tunes, surely it could sing back?

Thinking about the moon reminded PJ of something Ruth had said when they discussed the moonbow on their last time together in Mr. Splitzky's barn. What was it? *Nothing goes unnoticed in nature.*

Which meant everything Ruth had done with the birds and animals had found an even wider response in nature.

The late spring night became chillier, so PJ climbed into bed, but since she couldn't see the moon anymore, she pulled her candy-striped comforter and pillow off her bed and arranged them on the window seat. She could stretch full-out there and look up and see the moon looking back at her. As she drifted off she could swear she heard the flute music that Ruth loved.

Something startled her awake.

"*Pssst*, PJ?" Oohoo came hopping in the window and plopped right on top of her.

"Give me a break, Oohoo," said PJ, sitting up.

"We heard buzz on the birdvine about your art show coming up at school. What are you planning?"

"Oohoo, not now," PJ said wearily. "Can we talk about this during the weekend?"

"The guys are excited, PJ."

"Yeah, right. But these are early days, OK? I can't even draw anything at the moment."

"Ooooh, PJ, that's not good. How can we help?"

"I'll let you know. Thanks a bunch, Oohoo."

"OK, kiddo," Oohoo said reluctantly, and swooped back noisily into the night.

※

Mrs. Picklelime came home so early for the weekend that PJ was surprised to find her mom fixing coffee and baking biscuits in the kitchen for breakfast. It was before dawn!

Overjoyed, PJ hugged her tightly. "I've missed you, Mom."

Her mom kissed the top of her head. "Missed you, too, honey. More than you can imagine." Ruffling PJ's hair, she said, "I'm back for good now. Hey, you're beginning to get that wild look again. When did you last brush it?"

"C'mon, Mom," PJ giggled. "It's my trademark!"

"Well, I guess it beats tattoos or piercings."

They sat together and PJ shared everything she had been told since Ruth's death.

"Time helps make sense of things that seem overwhelming right now," said her mom. "At least it did for me."

"I feel angry, Mom. Why is an awful person like Mr. Tweety still around but Ruth isn't?"

"Why do you think?"

"I'd like to think it's because he needs to wind up in jail."

"Sounds good. At least his cruel business is ruined."

Thanks to Ruth, Josh, the gulls, and me, PJ thought. She got up to pour orange juice for them both.

Mrs. Picklelime watched her. "How are you and Dad doing, honey?"

PJ shrugged. "We keep the place clean and water the plants. We don't pig out on junk food, if that's what you mean." PJ lifted her head and listened. "I think he's still fast asleep."

"So, why don't we leave him hot biscuits and coffee

and take our breakfast down to the beach for some yoga together?"

"Great idea, Mom, only . . ." PJ looked at the clock. "Wait a minute. I'll be right back."

While her mom packed a picnic basket, PJ went to her room to get ready. After closing the door firmly, she changed into a fleecy orange hooded sweatsuit, opened her windows, curved her thumb and first finger against her lips, and gave several short, sharp whistles.

Within minutes, the barn owls and Oohoo—with Domino clinging to her—came flying across from Mr. Splitzky's barn and from one tree to the next until they landed on PJ's window ledge.

"Guys, I'd like you to meet my mom. We're going down to the beach. Why don't you and the gulls meet us near the waterfall?"

"Hooo. Way to go, PJ!" Oohoo said. Tyto and Monkey Face preened themselves and used one another's eyes as mirrors to tidy their feathers with their wing tips.

At that point, Squirt came leaping in from the pecan tree, determined to be included. PJ thought for a moment and then went to get the water-bottle carrier she used for cycling in the hot summer months. Its long cylindrical shape was perfect for transporting Squirt.

She waved goodbye to the owls and closed the window. "OK, Squirt. Here goes," she said. She picked him up, lowered him slowly into the carrier, and slung it over her shoulder.

When Mrs. Picklelime saw him, she chuckled and said, "Well at least you're not trying to hide him from me anymore!"

"You knew?" PJ said in surprise. Squirt popped his head out over the rim of the carrier and started his *brrrk-brrrkbrrrk*.

"Come on, PJ. Don't you think I did the same thing at your age?"

"Oh, Mom, why didn't you say something?"

Her mom laughed. "Oh no. That spoils the fun."

They packed the car with blankets, cushions, the picnic basket, and a thermos and drove out toward the clifftop as dawn began to break. Winds bit their cheeks and swayed the sea oats.

PJ and her mom hauled the picnic things down to the beach by Mrs. Patel's favorite waterfall. The tide was pulling out forcefully. It left long stretches of seaweed scattered across the wet sand. Sandpipers scurried about pecking furiously at tiny crabs.

They spread a blanket out, kicked off their sandals,

and started the sun salutation. As if on cue, a tiny curve of the sun's golden orb peeked over the horizon. With a flurry of beating wings, gulls swooped down from their nests in the cliffs. PJ raised a finger to her lips, as if to tell them that this was a silent exercise.

The birds encircled mother and daughter and bowed down in unison to repeat the sun salutation. Then others swooped down, including Oohoo, Domino, Monkey Face, Tyto, Big Gull, and Little Gull. Squirt jumped out of the water carrier and arched his back.

PJ had never seen the group like this. She then realized they *would* be different and more formal around her mother, of course, and not act out and talk over one another or goof about as they did with her.

Her mom didn't seem at all surprised to be surrounded by birds doing yoga exercises. Mrs. Patel had taught both PJ and her mom a few *asanas* in the garden, so maybe critters and bugs had been mimicking them then, too?

The birds and Squirt followed PJ's every move. They ended with the tree pose, standing on one leg with the other bent inward, wings or paws pressed together above their heads.

Suddenly one of the gulls toppled over and knocked

the next one, who knocked the next. Gull giggling and squawking and *caw-cawing* and funny owl sounds broke the silence. They all tumbled over one another and rolled around PJ until she wheeled right along with them.

Mrs. Picklelime cupped a hand over her mouth and said, "PJ, you're all making me seasick. I've never seen birds and squirrels behave like this anywhere!"

"Oh, come on, Mom! You told me you used to prowl around at night watching raccoons and so on. Didn't they goof about for you?"

"Well, not like *this*." She laughed. *"Birds frolic in time like fools in sand, wind, and brine, but only for you, PJ, my little Sunshine Picklelime."*

"Oh, Mom, stop. You embarrass me." PJ blushed. "Do they teach you poetry along with counseling?"

Her mom smiled and reached into the basket for their breakfast. Realizing she was surrounded by many pairs of hungry eyes, Mrs. Picklelime opened a bag of birdseed and began tossing the seeds around the circle.

As if from nowhere, dozens of birds materialized and swooped down to share the feast, grabbing seeds from under the beaks of others. Mrs. Picklelime rose, but PJ touched her arm. "It's OK, Mom. I packed plenty, just move back a little." She sat next to her mom on the blanket and they shared fruit salad and warm biscuits and blackberry jam. Mrs. Picklelime poured herself a steaming cup of coffee, and orange juice for PJ.

PJ threw chunks of biscuit in the air. Gulls rose, snapping bits in midflight. Squirt jumped up to catch pieces they dropped.

Mrs. Picklelime got up after a while and said she felt like stretching her legs, so PJ packed away the breakfast things in the basket. As soon as her mom was out of earshot, she turned to her friends.

"You guys were magnificent," she said as they clustered around her.

"I could have done without *them*," snorted Big Gull, nodding his head toward two large black crows. "*Sooooo* noisy! And look at those cruel hard beaks jutting out between those beady little crow eyes!"

"Big Gull, you surprise me," said PJ. "Everyone's welcome here!"

"Yeah, c'mon, BG, where's your community spirit, you old buzzard?" Little Gull piped up.

PJ lifted her head and glanced over at the big crows. "Crow friends? Come and meet the gang."

The crows looked at one another and back at PJ. "You

mean us?" one asked, his large beak snapping open and shut like a trapdoor.

"Sure. Come and join us!"

They walked over slowly, one foot planted warily in the sand after the other. "Charles Crow the Third. Just call me Chuck," said the bigger one, extending a black wing tip to PJ.

"Cathy Crow the First. Just call me Cathy," chortled the other crow.

"Are you guys together?" PJ asked.

"We are," they chorused.

PJ introduced them all around and invited them to join their next beach-yoga session. The crows thanked her but said they were "just passing through" and needed to continue on their journey, miles up the coast, to a forest of spruce and maple where several of their grown-up chicks lived. Then, black wings spread out, they said goodbye and lifted off heavily from the beach, leaving huge claw prints in the sand.

"Guess I misjudged them," said Big Gull, head tilted back as he watched the crows fly higher and higher.

"*I'm* sorry they've gone," Domino piped up suddenly. Everyone looked at the baby magpie in surprise. "I'm the only little black-and-white guy around and I liked looking at them," he said as the crows shrank to tiny dots in the sky.

Oohoo wrapped Domino in her wings and held him close to her chest. "Hey, ink spot. I'm every color of brown, won't I do?"

"I guess so," Domino said, his funny little voice all muffled against Oohoo's soft feathers.

"Get real, kiddo!" added Big Gull. "We're also half and half," he said. He twitched his polka-dot tail.

Squirt began cartwheeling around the circle to show off his gray fur. He jumped onto PJ's shoulder and draped himself around her neck like a scarf.

PJ spotted her mother wandering toward them, trailing a length of seaweed behind her. "OK, gang," said PJ, "what's this I hear about a bunch of gulls chasing Helicopter Pete out of town?"

Big Gull and Little Gull made a great show of looking from left to right and cawing over one another, "What?" "Who?" and "What's this neighborhood coming to?"

PJ chucked them playfully under their beaks. "You guys. Don't get too reckless," she said, mimicking Mrs. Patel's advice to her. Then she said, "Let's keep this short. You wanted to talk about the art show?"

They all ooohed and cawed in agreement.

"You've given me great ideas today," she said, and shared some suggestions they all liked. "But keep it a secret. Off you go, then, gang. Let's see what you can do."

Her bird friends hopped and bounced off along the beach and into the sky, where they dipped and swirled above mischievously, practicing some yoga twists in midair. Mrs. Picklelime stopped in her tracks and framed them with her hands as though capturing a private snapshot.

"PJ, your drawings are beginning to make more sense to me," she said.

PJ held her breath, reluctant to say anything about her creative block after such a perfect morning. She rose and began shaking sand off the blanket while her mom collected the rest of their things.

"What about Squirt?" Mrs. Picklelime eyed the squirrel, still draped around her daughter's neck. "Is he going home with us like that?"

"Of course!" said PJ, tugging his tail. "Aren't I nicer than the water-bottle carrier?"

CHAPTER 13

blackbirds

Mrs. Patel found PJ in the back garden, frantically spinning the compost bins around and around. "Child, stop. You're making the earthworms dizzy," she said, tilting her head from side to side.

"I need to do crazy things, Mrs. Patel."

"How so?"

PJ took a step back. The bin continued to swing to and fro for a few minutes. "I still can't seem to sketch anymore."

"PJ, that's enough. Go and change and wash your face and hands. Evi Lenz has invited us to watch her make a new batch of Lemon Nectar truffles. I have slivers of lemon peel for her right here," she said, holding up a bag.

"But I'm—"

"No buts, PJ. I'll wait for you at the front gate."

Ten minutes later, PJ appeared in ripped jeans, a huge T-shirt fashioned out of recycled sugar sacks, and sandals shaped out of old car tires. Expecting Mrs. Patel to say something like, What will you wear next, child? she was surprised when Mrs. Patel nodded her approval and said, "Aha, much better."

Off they went on foot to the Dream. They arrived just as Ms. Lenz lifted the cover off a large pot of melted white chocolate on a hot plate at the back of the shop. A sweeter-than-usual fragrance filled the air.

"Oh, perfect timing, Shanti and PJ. Come over here and watch me," she said. She thanked them for the lemon slivers and emptied the bag into a special shaker. She placed the slivers next to her other tools—a funnel, corn flour, and little silver forks—all lined up on wax paper covering a large silver tray beside the hot plate.

She explained that handmade truffles had to be crafted very carefully according to temperature, to make sure the semisoft truffle filling mix of chocolate and lemon nectar did not fall apart when dipped in melted chocolate.

"Before we dip balls of chocolate-and-lemon-nectar mix in here," she said, stirring the pot of warm white chocolate, "I have to make sure the consistency is just right."

They watched wide-eyed as Ms. Lenz brought a slab of the mix from a cool spot in her shop and placed it on the wax paper. To PJ, it looked like a block of white fudge. Ms. Lenz scooped out a generous tablespoonful and squeezed it through the funnel to create the perfect size for the first truffle.

"My hands have to be dry and not too warm," she said. So she patted corn flour on her hands before rolling the young truffle into a smooth ball between her palms. She then stuck the tiny silver forks into either end of the truffle, dipped it in the pot of thick liquid chocolate, and placed it on the wax paper.

Finally she shaped the surface with the forks, sprinkled the truffle with lemon peel, and let it cool while she prepared a second truffle.

Nodding at the two little lemon truffles and then at PJ and Mrs. Patel, she said, "Go ahead, ladies. Those are for you."

"Brilliant," said PJ as she popped one in her mouth. It dissolved faster than anything she had tasted before. The tiny lemon-peel slivers tickled her tongue.

"Goodness," said Mrs. Patel, fanning herself. "Quite intoxicating! My, oh my, Evi. Sure you haven't added anything stronger than lemon to the mix?"

Ms. Lenz laughed and shook her head. Her copper curls bounced around, and PJ really did hear bells ringing.

Once they'd recovered from the shock of tasting freshly made truffles, Mrs. Patel helped to squeeze the mix through the funnel, Ms. Lenz rolled the raw truffle between her palms, and PJ used the little forks to dip and shape it.

As the trio worked together in harmony, Ms. Lenz explained that people like her who came from a long line of chocolatiers took special care of the tools of their craft. "We call this cooking pot *trampier*," she said. Holding up the little silver fork, she added, "And this is the *trampier-gabel*."

She showed PJ how to use the fork to "pockmark" some of the truffles to look like little lemons, as a variation on those sprinkled with peel.

The fragrance of white chocolate and lemon became even more intense. PJ studied the rows of perfect truffles. The circular shapes reminded her of the stepping stones in Ms. Naguri's garden. "Ms. Lenz," she said suddenly, "do you meditate when you make truffles?"

Again, more laughter. "I like working calmly and consistently," she explained. "Yes, anything you do over and over to try and achieve perfection is meditative. Today it's different." She began to place several truffles in a special box. "I'm taking these to Ruth's parents. They've sat shiva—that's a week of mourning when friends and family join them in daily prayer in their home. Everyone brought food. But it's time I brought them something sweet. It's traditional in my family."

"You mean these truffles are sort of . . . blessed, Ms. Lenz?" PJ asked.

"Perhaps, yes," she agreed. "Ruth is in my heart right now."

"Then no 'perhaps' about it!" Mrs. Patel said. "The truffles *are* blessed."

Tears began to prickle PJ's eyelids. She tried to brush them away.

"It's perfectly OK to cry, child," Mrs. Patel said.

"We have all lost someone who is dear to us," Ms. Lenz said. "But there are *always* others who need our friendship just as much."

"And need your chocolate, too, Evi," Mrs. Patel added, helping herself to another truffle and offering one to PJ.

PJ closed her eyes, remembering the day she took lemon truffles to Ruth and Josh. The truffle melting in her mouth right now tasted totally different. It seemed to fill her ears and her whole head and lift her feet off the ground. She couldn't speak. It was comforting to be with two adults who didn't expect her to say anything.

Evi Lenz touched PJ's cheek. "Mrs. Patel says you do wonderful pastels. Bring your sketch pad here next time?" Pointing at the formal pictures of chocolates on the walls, she said, "Boring, aren't they? I'm a rebel, PJ. I want you to draw dancing truffles, singing truffles, mountain-climbing truffles, flying truffles, truffles on bicycles. Bring them alive for me!"

PJ hesitated. What if she couldn't deliver? "Are you serious, Ms. Lenz?" she asked.

"I *am* serious," said Evi Lenz. "No rush. Think of this as your summer job."

"Wow," was all PJ could say.

"Not too fast with your 'wowing,' PJ," said Mrs. Patel. "Your art project for school comes first, remember? Off we go now, child, or your parents will complain Evi and I have ruined your appetite with sweeties!"

PJ couldn't wait for art class to be able to tell her teacher Mr. Santos about the Chocolate Dream and the request from Evi Lenz. Surely her block would lift by summer?

All morning she could hear him singing Spanish love songs at the top of his rich tenor voice in the studio down the hall, so it was hard for her to concentrate on earlier classes in history and English.

In fact, both Mr. Santos and Mr. Flax, the botany teacher, were busily preparing a large empty space in the big studio for the students' upcoming end-of-semester art show that PJ now knew was to be titled Art in Nature and Nature in Art.

Groups of students in art or botany had been given wall and display space to do whatever they chose, new works or a collection of works completed during the semester. Themes had to link art and nature in any creative way.

After discussing the project with both Mr. Santos and Mr. Flax, PJ felt inspired to create a sort of storybook presentation of her drawings, starting off with the discovery of Lemon Pie in the yellow rosebush and ending with the tree house and the other birds. At least she could use her existing sketches and not risk being unable to draw anything new.

When she told Mr. Santos about Joshua's camcording adventures, he suggested they work on a mixed-media presentation in Ruth's honor.

Joshua said by phone, "In Ruth's honor? Oh, PJ, if only she could see it and enjoy it!"

"I know," said PJ. "But it's also for you and your folks."

Joshua had missed so much school because of Ruth's death that he was still trying to catch up. He apologized to PJ since she had to do most of the preparation.

PJ shrugged this off. Perhaps it was best if she worked out her creative blocks on her own, anyway.

During class, Mr. Santos asked PJ how she would like to display her artwork. "You have a choice, PJ," he said. "Freestanding display boards? Or a scrim?"

"Scrim?" asked PJ, puzzled.

"That huge canvas hanging over there," he said, pointing at some scenery showing a view of a house and a brick wall, salvaged from a school play staged the year before.

"Maybe the scrim, Mr. Santos," she said, not entirely convinced this was the best choice. She studied it and tried to see how it might be used. "Can I paint over it?" she asked.

"Of course, PJ."

PJ wondered how she could do this. Throw pots of paint at it and step back to see the results? Take a random choice of colors and sponge over them? Or to be safe, should she simply use the leftover yellow paint from her room? She had to think about this.

When PJ cycled home later, her mind seesawed between ideas that felt great one minute and dumb the next. She was so caught up in her thoughts, she didn't notice a sudden wind at first. It seemed to gust in from the sea. Branches swayed. Tins and bottles rolled noisily along the sidewalks. Sea spray trickled down PJ's cheeks and she had to stop for a minute to dry her hands on her jeans.

Above, flocks of blackbirds lined up on the electric wires as far as the eye could see and then swooped down and swooped up in a bizarre U formation. PJ stopped and watched them. They were noisy and unfamiliar, and smaller than the crows she'd met on the beach.

Were they bringing some sort of message? Was there another oil spill? Or were pirate ships busily hijacking cargo boats out in the bay?

The wind became too strong for her to cycle, so she wheeled her bike the rest of the way home. She hoped her bird friends might swing by to bring news of some kind. But her lawn and window ledge were bare. No one responded to her sharp whistles. Not even Squirt was out there, swinging from one branch to the next. She just had to be patient.

PJ spent the late afternoon unpinning her drawings from the corkboard. She slipped them between the pages of a firm drawing block to keep them nice and flat to transport to school the next day.

She also finally decided to use her leftover yellow paint for the scrim, so she trotted downstairs to ask her dad for the drop cloths, rollers, and tray.

"Are you kids painting the school?" he asked, lowering his newspaper.

PJ explained the upcoming project.

"Sounds interesting, but art doesn't put beans on the table, PJ. Don't get fancy ideas for the future from this project, will you?"

"Dad, this summer I *can* put beans on the table," PJ said, and started to tell him about the request from Ms. Lenz.

"That's great, PJ," he cut in.

PJ could see his mind was miles away, so she left it at that.

There was nothing on the evening news about the swarms of blackbirds passing overhead. The image kept bothering PJ, so she returned to her room, hoping one of her bird friends would hop in and update her. No such luck.

The blackbirds had looked like a dark cloud announcing something, but what? Later that night, PJ found out. The wind began to howl. Lightning split the sky and lit up her room. Rain slashed down and hit her window-panes with such force that when PJ opened them and put her head out, the rain stung her cheeks. Below, the bamboo fountain filled up with water and started to snap back and forth.

Within moments, Squirt came hurtling onto the ledge. He hopped inside, cold and bedraggled. His tail was so wet and skinny, it made him look like a big rat. PJ dried him and tried to fluff his fur, but all he wanted to do was jump into his tartan-lined box and curl up in a ball.

PJ continued to listen to the storm. Rain rushed along the gutters. It made her feel so restless, she swung her legs out the window and slid down the trellis to the sodden flower bed below. She landed with a squelch.

PJ jumped around in the mud, imagining herself in a batch of chocolate truffle mix. Rain flattened her pajamas against her body and soaked her to the skin in seconds.

She ran onto the lawn and began spinning in circles. The movement reminded her of the way she spun around in Ruth's tree house for the first time.

She started to cry. Everything that had been bottled up inside her for days came bursting out. She lay face-down on the lawn and covered her head with her arms. The long, wet grass felt soft and sweet against her face.

"PJ, what are you *doing*?"

She rolled over to find her mom kneeling beside her in a slicker.

"Come on, honey," Mrs. Picklelime said, taking her daughter in her arms.

"Mom, I'm OK," PJ sobbed.

"I know what this is about. Come inside. You'll catch pneumonia if you stay out here." She lifted PJ off the grass and walked her through the front door, straight into the kitchen. She wrapped her in a huge beach towel and dried her vigorously.

After tossing the towel in the wash, she cocooned PJ in a soft wool blanket and heated up some milk for them both.

"I couldn't seem to cry before now," PJ said, stirring the froth on top of her milk.

"Don't worry, baby, that's normal. You'll go through all sorts of highs and lows over the next weeks. It's important to talk about this."

"I don't feel good talking to you or Dad," PJ admitted. "You have your own problems. I don't even like being in the house when you're here at the same time."

"I know, PJ. I'm so sorry. We're working on a solution for all our sakes. This won't take long, I promise you." Mrs. Picklelime reached out and held her daughter's hands for a long time.

Comforted by her mother's warmth, PJ had no need to say anything more. She leaned across the table, kissed and hugged her mom good night, and went upstairs to her room.

Still wrapped in the soft wool blanket, she sat on her window seat, reached for her pad and pastels, and sketched. And sketched. Her hand could hardly keep up with the images that tumbled out of her imagination. She nodded off just before dawn, listening to the dripping trees and the *plink-plonk* of the bamboo fountain below.

During art class the next day, PJ—well prepared in her now totally paint-crusted jeans and T-shirt—spread out the drop cloths carefully and arranged her tray and rollers so no one would trip over them.

The other kids busied themselves with their own personal displays of art and sculpture. Mr. Santos left them to their creativity, only giving a helping hand when asked.

Using long sweeping movements, PJ began to transform the scrim into the yellow backdrop she wanted for her artwork. The roller went *swish, swish,* and she needed a ladder to reach the top. The final yellow wasn't exactly the same as her room color. But it was a bright sunny spot that caught her eye wherever she stood in the large studio.

PJ took a step back when the scrim was finished and studied it carefully. Something was missing. She took another step back, hands on hips.

"What is it, PJ?" Mr. Santos asked.

PJ touched the surface. "It's just not enough to hang my pictures here."

"Ah, PJ, sketch whatever is running around in your mind on paper to give you a sense of scale. Then draw vertical and horizontal lines around the images for a grid," Mr. Santos advised, tapping one hand at right angles to the other to show her. "Later, apply that to the scrim."

"I want to be freer, Mr. Santos. Not tied to a grid!" said PJ.

"*Claro*, PJ! But the grid will free you."

"How? It sounds so stiff."

"PJ, come on. Give it form, life. A house could be a grid. So could a wooden fence. So could a tall tree."

"A *tree*? YES!" PJ shouted out loud. "Ruth's live oak. Of course!"

Classmates all over the studio turned and looked at her in surprise.

"*Muy bien!*" Mr. Santos said. "You'll find extra brown and green paint in the storeroom, PJ. Help yourself."

☀

Before PJ tackled the grid, she cycled over to Ruth's home and sketched the tree house in its huge live oak host. Soon, Mr. Splitzky would transport it to the Picklelimes' own garden.

In the morning, she went to school very early to get started. She placed her sketch on an easel for quick reference and began to paint the "grid" of the huge live oak to fill the entire canvas. The lowest branches almost touched the ground. She painted the largest branches across to the edge of the canvas like some curvy mythical sea creature destined to keep growing on and on. She also painted clusters of small, dark green leaves. Finally she painted the tree house resting on two branches and nestled against the mighty trunk.

PJ squared her shoulders, took a deep breath, and painted an image of Ruth in her purple T-shirt leaning over the lower half of the door, thick, honey-blond pigtail dangling. PJ's heart began to beat triple-time. Powerful noises surrounded her as other kids began to fill up the studio to complete their own projects. As an afterthought, she painted Squirt encircling Ruth's neck, his long bushy tail in full bloom. Of all the rescue pets, Squirt was the closest to Ruth. PJ painted his fur to match Ruth's eyes.

The effect was beautiful. PJ reached for her other sketches to attach to the branches. She used double-sided tape to avoid hurting the canvas and her artwork. First she attached Lemon Pie on the far left. She stood and stared at him for a long time. Then she took him down and reached for the pot of yellow paint. It didn't seem right somehow just to hang him there and remove him later. She had an urge to paint him on a branch, peeking out of the dark green leaves. She wanted Lemon Pie and Ruth to be a permanent part of the canvas.

As she daubed splashes of yellow and cream to bring her dear bird buddy alive, head back, beak open, and singing his funny little tune, PJ knew in that instant she would never see him again. There was no reason, no logical reason. She just knew.

Ruth was right. At some point PJ had to let go, to stop hankering, hoping. She just had to keep him alive in her imagination.

Since Lemon Pie was the first bird in her rescue story, PJ painted a much bigger version of him to be sure everyone noticed the warbler. Then, in sequence, she began attaching her other pictures. Sometimes she paused to paint an image directly on the canvas of something she had almost forgotten, such as the gulls flying off like musical notes into the distant sky. Cardy and Mrs. Cardy made beautiful splashes of red on a dark branch above the tree house against the yellow backdrop.

PJ added her images of Big Gull, Little Gull, the Gull Gang, and Messenger Gull as they dipped, swirled, and swooped in from some far-off cliffside.

Then came the owls. PJ studied her various drawings

and decided she needed fresher images, so she put the owl drawings to one side and reached for assorted pots of brown, white, and gray paints. She clustered the owls together on the twisting branch that supported the left side of the tree house. Tyto and Monkey Face contrasted with mottled Oohoo and funny little black-and-white Domino.

PJ folded her arms, stepped back, and assessed her work. The yellow backdrop made the collage of the huge live oak, the tree house, and the collection of pictures vibrate with life.

A quick-action replay of images kept jumping into her imagination, like the magical moonbow. She lined up all the colors and dabbed them in arcs in sequence from memory. Finally, with the help of a ladder, she added a shimmering moon to the top right-hand corner.

"Aaaaaaah, *bravo!*" Mr. Santos said. "You have made the live oak sing, PJ, sing!" He cupped one hand behind his ear. "Listen how the wind whispers through the branches!"

PJ listened, but still, she felt something was missing. Then it hit her. Of course! She reached for cream and gold paints. Blossom!

She painted the retriever standing upright with his

paws against the trunk, head back, barking happily up at Ruth. His caramel color almost matched Squirt's belly and the flecks in Ruth's eyes.

Now all they needed was Josh's video. PJ went off to look for a high stool for his laptop so everything would be ready for him when he arrived.

CHAPTER 14

the art show

PJ was doing laundry when her father came home from work.

"Is Mom here?" he asked.

"No. Not yet." PJ removed clothes from the dryer and began folding and separating them in piles.

"I'm moving out soon," he said shortly.

PJ wasn't surprised. In fact, it was something of a relief. "I know you're not happy here," she said. "Why pretend everything's OK? Where will you go?"

"I'm looking at apartments closer to work," he told her. "We'll plan regular visits. I'm not going to disappear!"

"I know," she said. "I'm so sorry, Dad."

"It's not your fault, PJ."

Reluctant to get into a deeper discussion, PJ said, "Are you coming to the art show opening at school?"

"Is your mother going?"

"Of course."

"Then it's best if I don't go," her dad answered.

PJ noticed her father's expression and said, "Would you like a sneak preview? I'll ask Mr. Santos. I know he'll say yes."

"OK, thanks, PJ. That might work," he said.

"Dad?"

"PJ?"

"These are yours." She smiled and handed him his shirts, all neatly folded.

☀

When the art studio opened its doors to parents and members of the public on the great day, it was wall-to-wall people. During the first hour, in Ruth's honor, Josh and his parents, PJ, her mom, Mrs. Patel, Ms. Naguri, Ms. Lenz, Mr. Splitzky, Mrs. Martins, Mr. Santos, Mr. Flax, other neighbors, and all Ruth's closest buddies stood in silence in front of PJ's splashy yellow canvas with the massive live oak, tree house, and collection of birds and animals. Ruth's image also faced them in a frozen frame on Josh's laptop, perched on a high stool by the wall. Mr. Santos announced that the canvas would continue to hang in the front entrance to the school after the exhibition closed, as a permanent tribute to Ruth.

There were hugs and tears and neighborly words of appreciation all around. PJ watched sadly as Ruth's parents started to go, after telling her Mr. Splitzky planned to dismantle the tree house and bring it to her garden the next day.

"Are you sure?" PJ asked.

"It's time," they said, and Joshua nodded in agreement.

He remained behind after they left and said he felt really close to Ruth, standing next to her image on the canvas. He adjusted the laptop to show a continuous loop of his clips of the birds—and the escape.

Everyone stood and gaped in disbelief, eyes darting between PJ's collage and the moving images as dozens of birds dumped all over Mr. Tweety on the sidewalk beside his poop-smeared store windows. "Hey, didn't we see that on the TV news?" someone exclaimed. "Wow, talk about timing, Josh! Were you just passing by?"

"Something like that." He shrugged, shaking his shaggy honey-blond hair so it tumbled over his face and masked his expression.

When people asked more questions, PJ stood there trying to look innocent in her flowing turquoise linen skirt and shirt with a ladybug motif, chosen to add to the nature-and-art project. Beside her, Joshua looked like some rare tropical bird in his deep crimson T-shirt and jeans.

Out of respect for the family, music only started after Ruth's parents left. Teachers from the music and electronics departments had set up a sound system, not so loud that people couldn't hear themselves speak. All those kids exhibiting their art got to pick a piece of music. PJ and Josh chose Ruth's favorite jazz flute music, and it blended in smoothly with classical, pop, and heavy metal.

Proud parents and guests drifted from exhibit to exhibit, quizzing the students about their choices and congratulating them on their creativity. The art included pen-and-ink botanical drawings, exotic wood carvings, and time-lapse photographs of butterflies emerging from cocoons. After the recent cleanup days on the beach, some students created great works of sculpture shaped out of shells and salvaged objects like plastic sandals and weathered bits of old crab traps.

Some of the younger kids dressed up in animal or flower costumes. One was even dressed as a mushroom. They wandered around with platters of halved pineapples filled with fresh papaya, melon, kiwifruit, and grapes.

PJ couldn't wait any longer to spring her surprise as a final tribute to Ruth. Mr. Santos didn't know about it. Nor did Mr. Flax.

The gulls, owls, and cardinals danced about and flapped wildly with excitement at an upper window, awaiting her cue.

While the place was still packed, PJ reached up for the cord and yanked open the window. Down swooped the birds. Folks ducked, fearing a replay of what they had just seen in Joshua's video clips. PJ held her breath.

Big Gull couldn't resist flying so close he tweaked PJ's hair. He started to *caw-caw*, and that set the owls off, too, with their assortment of hissing and hooting. Then the Cardies started their lovely *chirruping*. The birds began to twirl and dip in formation and make figures-of-eight like an air force display. Then they started doing yoga poses in flight.

Suddenly people weren't diving for cover anymore,

but watched, enchanted, and clapped and cheered. Everyone thought this was an organized part of the art show.

"Phenomenal," someone said to Mr. Flax and Mr. Santos.

PJ made a quick thumbs-up sign no one noticed except Josh. The birds rose in unison, dipped, frolicked, tumbled, spun around, flew back to their perch above, and then out the window. The crowd roared.

Though PJ tried to keep a cool expression throughout, her mom, Josh, Mrs. Patel, and Ms. Lenz smiled and winked at her. People buzzed around the floor talking about the display and asking, "Who trained the birds?" and "Have you ever seen owls and a magpie flying with seagulls and cardinals before?" Even little Domino had separated himself from Oohoo to twirl about solo.

After everything had simmered down, guests began to make their way to the dessert table. Parents had baked delicious cakes and pies for the occasion. Ms. Lenz had made a huge chocolate slab cake decorated with owls. Ms. Naguri had made a pecan cake. Mr. Splitzky had baked a honey cake shaped like a beehive.

At the end of the show, Mr. Santos and Mr. Flax helped PJ and Josh move the canvas to its permanent place at the front of the school. When PJ got home, exhausted, she wasn't surprised to find the birds and Squirt waiting for her.

"Guys, you were *awesome*," she said. PJ felt something tighten around her heart and could hardly breathe for a moment. Tears seemed to spiral up from a hidden place inside she didn't even know she had. The birds drew close, opened their wings, and formed a tight circle around her. PJ had always been so supportive of them, Oohoo murmured, maybe they had lost sight of her feelings?

"PJ, we all love you," sniffed Big Gull, salty tears flowing down his beak. "We're your family."

She nodded but found it impossible to speak. Part of her wanted to freeze this moment in time and never grow up. Part of her never wanted the birds and Squirt to leave, but she knew that was impossible. Part of her wanted to speed through these days.

"Tomorrow," said PJ, "the tree house moves here and I expect you guys to start scouting around for injured birds and animals to fill those empty cages."

"You got it, PJ!" everyone chorused.

The circle of wings tightened around her and then released as the birds lifted off the ledge one by one and returned to the folds of the inky night sky.

CHAPTER 15

pj's tree house

PJ awoke very early the next morning to hear her mother dragging furniture around the front room. She got dressed in apple green shorts and a T-shirt and ran downstairs to find out what was going on.

"Hi, honey," said Mrs. Picklelime. "What do you think? I'm converting this room into my office. Soon I'll start seeing patients here." Then, stretching her arms and legs, she added, "As poet Audre Lorde said, *'If I didn't define myself for myself, I would be crunched into other people's fantasies for me and eaten alive.'* "

"Oh, Mom, you're uncrunchable. Room looks great. Anyway, we spend most of our time in the kitchen."

"It's cozier there, sure. We won't miss being in here. I'll move a desk and filing cabinets in soon, too."

She had arranged a ring of chairs to face the large window, circled by bookshelves crammed full of her favorite writers and poets. The window gave a wonderful view of the garden and their own smaller version of a twisty live oak that would soon hold the tree house.

"The garden's growing lovelier by the day, PJ," she said. "But make sure you keep the front lawn free of bird poop. Oh, and PJ?"

"Mom?"

"I do not want to see birds and squirrels flying around inside the house, especially when I'm seeing patients. Confine them to the tree house or your window ledge. Is that clear?"

"Yes, Mom." PJ grinned, kissed her on the cheek, and ran outside just as Mrs. Patel opened the front gate.

"Come, child," she said. "Mr. Splitzky will be at Ruth's place within the hour to take the tree house apart and truck it here to you. Let's go there and wait for him."

As they walked together, Mrs. Patel congratulated PJ again on the art exhibit. "PJ, when you said 'mixed media,' you didn't tell me this included an overhead show!"

"That just happened, Mrs. Patel," PJ said.

"Oh, right. You know, child, your birds will pass on whatever they learn from you to their offspring. Never forget that. But birds need to be birds. Don't baby them too much."

"I'll try not to." PJ laughed.

"I wanted to share something with you," Mrs. Patel went on as they turned the corner. "Mozart sometimes spent his summer vacations in a house just outside Prague. That's where—so they say—he started to compose one of his operas, out in the garden. You know how I love gardens? Years ago I sat in that garden at a stone table and listened to the birds, oh wonderful birds, PJ, you cannot imagine how beautiful. And I thought to myself, these are the great-great-great-great a hundred times over grandchildren of the birds that sang right here in this same spot for Mozart!"

"Did they sound like Mozart?"

Mrs. Patel nodded. "I think we're told one of his works was inspired by songbirds he heard outside his window."

PJ loved the idea and told Mrs. Patel about the gulls flying off into the distance looking like musical notes.

When they got to Ruth's, they crossed the lawn, now full of white rain lilies after the recent storm. All they could hear was the sound of the stone fountain with a girl holding a pot. They stood in silence for several long moments, staring at the huge, winding live oak and the tree house, until Joshua poked his head out the door and said, "Yo! Just in time to help. Catch these?" He lowered the empty animal cages down, all carefully roped together. PJ and Mrs. Patel carried them over to the gate as Mr. Splitzky drove up in his truck with three beefy-looking workmen.

Josh tossed down one puffy blue cushion after another. Mrs. Patel and Mr. Splitzky loaded all the items behind the driver's seat in the truck while PJ swung up the ladder for a few words with Joshua. Together they put some of Ruth's books and pictures into a box he wanted to keep for himself. "PJ, don't look so worried," he said. "I'm OK with this. I'm working through things. Yester-day's show helped a lot."

"It did?" PJ asked.

"Sure. I felt Ruth was there with us."

"I don't feel she's ever left," said PJ.

Since Mr. Splitzky was waiting below, they quickly emptied the tree house and lowered the rest of the items so he could begin the dismantling process. First he unhinged the door and lowered it to their upturned hands. Then he removed the windows. He'd built the tree house in practical sections, so he took those apart and slid each one down, helped by his trio of workmen.

Mrs. Picklelime soon came over to help. As a team, they started to load the sections into the back of Mr. Splitzky's truck, taking extra care to pack the windows between protective sheets of foam.

As soon as the tree house was down, PJ called Ms. Naguri, who walked over to hang up the bamboo wood chimes. A breeze caught them immediately and twirled them to and fro in a dance of sound. Everyone could hear them *clickclacking* as the team finished loading and ambled back to the Picklelimes' garden.

Other neighbors were waiting there with picnic baskets all prepared. They made the off-loading easier. Many pairs of hands helped Mr. Splitzky raise and reassemble the tree house in PJ's live oak. PJ wished they could build a walkway from her bedroom right into the tree house, but her mom said, "Don't even think about it."

PJ and Josh organized the interior with all the cushions, cages, and shelves in their former places.

"PJ? Josh?" Mrs. Picklelime called from below. "We're hungry!"

PJ poked her head over the Dutch door. "We'll be there in two minutes, Mom."

Neighbors were busily spreading blankets on the grass and opening their picnic hampers. Mrs. Patel went home to get fresh pitchers of Lemon Nectar sweetened with Mr. Splitzky's honey. Mr. Santos unpacked large green Spanish olives and placed them in a bowl he'd shaped out of limestone. Mr. Kanafani unwrapped loaves of flatbread he'd baked specially. Mrs. Martins arrived with an avocado salad. Ms. Naguri brought some of her famous sushi, and Ms. Lenz came with a large box of truffles and pralines.

Mr. Splitzky had made an extra gift for PJ. It was a bird feeder, a mini version of the tree house, which he dangled from a branch of the pecan tree. It swayed in a new, salty breeze that seemed to join them straight from the ocean.

Squirt suddenly came leaping between the branches and plopped down on the lawn by Joshua's feet. Denied the flight show performed by the birds the day before, he seemed determined to stage his own show.

To everyone's delight, he spun about, doing a series of cartwheels, and ended up in Mr. Santos's olives.

Covered in oil, he rolled around on the grass and then shot up the pecan tree and slid down the chain, straight into the bird feeder. Josh rose to crumble some of Mr. Kanafani's bread for him.

"That rascal Squirt," said Mrs. Picklelime. "Come fall he'll be cracking pecans and burying them in the garden for winter!"

All eyes were on the squirrel. He twisted in the bird feeder. When it swayed dizzily on the long chain, he took a flying leap into the tree house.

Neighbors only began to clear up and leave around sunset, when the sky turned all shades of soft pink and deep red. As they left, the birds flew into the garden and through the open windows of the tree house.

PJ and Josh climbed the ladder to join them. They all clustered around to watch the sunset darken through the skylight.

"Tree house feels at home here, doesn't it, PJ?" Josh punched one of the big, puffy blue cushions. "Ruth would approve. She'd also expect me to help you with the gang." He high-fived Squirt, the gulls, and the owls. "Call me when you're ready."

"We will, Josh. And soon."

Squirt and the birds watched as the two hugged good-bye.

Josh slid down the ladder and then stood at the foot of the tree and said, "PJ, can I adopt you as my new sister?"

"Only if I can adopt you as my brother!"

He looked up at her for a long time as if reluctant to leave, and then walked away, turning back every few moments to wave.

PJ wondered why she couldn't stop watching him as he unlatched the front gate. Then she realized why. When he wasn't goofing about, Josh looked even more like Ruth.

"Whooooo," said Oohoo, fanning herself. "He's *cute*! Listen, PJ. Domino and I are moving out of Mr. Splitzky's barn. We'll find a little place for ourselves in this live oak. We need to keep an eye on you!"

"Oh, don't be silly, Oohoo!"

Loud hoots and *caw-caws* and wing slapping rocked the tree house.

"C'mon, guys, give me a break," said PJ.

Big Gull hopped onto the windowsill and said, "Oohoo and Domino aren't the only ones moving in, PJ. Cardy and Mrs. Cardy are nesting in your corner rose-bush where you taught Lemon Pie to sing."

"I thought I heard them *chirpchirping* earlier." PJ smiled.

Little Gull piped up. "Gang? I think we should split now and visit tomorrow. You too, Squirt. Been a long day, and PJ looks as though she needs time alone here."

They surrounded PJ and hugged and said noisy farewells to one another and lifted off as quickly as they had flown in. Squirt was the last to leave.

PJ hung over the door and watched them disappear into the warm night. Dozens of fireflies darted about below, a sure sign they were on the edge of summer.

There was so much to look forward to now.

PJ could smell the rosemary bushes and imagined what it would be like when the air was heavy with jasmine. The garden was beginning to take shape beautifully, and compost was breaking down slowly in the tumbler bins at the back. Rain barrels were full following the recent storm.

PJ thanked Ruth silently in her heart.

Next time Josh visited, they'd play some flute music to the birds.

Soon they could watch the moon change from a circle of clear ice into a perfect crescent surrounded by stars, and on into the large golden strawberry moon of summer.

acknowledgments

PJ Picklelime was born during lunches of cheese-and-pickle sandwiches and breakfasts of toast and lime marmalade with Debra Duncan Persinger, PhD, while we crafted our anthology *Sand to Sky: Conversations with Teachers of Asian Medicine*, published in 2008. Both Debra and I had the sort of crazily untamable hair that was once the despair of our respective mothers. When I joked about our hair as a perfect bird's nest, out popped PJ and chapter one. Thank you, Debra, for stirring my imagination.

My appreciation also goes to Susy Kiefer of Basel, Switzerland, for her chocolate knowledge and the opportunity to step into the kitchen of her favorite Kaffi Zum König, owned by the Gilgen brothers, to observe Peter Gilgen engaged in the fine art of truffle making.

Thank you, Jennifer Arena of Random House, for your inspiring editing and for helping me bring out the very best of PJ. Thank you, art director Tracy Tyler and illustrator Christian Slade, for your super interpretations.

I'm equally blessed with wonderful agents: Edythea Ginis Selman (New York), David Grossman (London), and Ruth Weibel (Zurich)—all of whom have given me years of encouragement and support.

My great soul sisters Bernadette Winiker, Sophie Keir, and Nancy Casey have given me incredible support through decades of writing and teaching and have offered insightful advice through several drafts of my books.

My appreciation goes to Miriam Hood of Austin, Texas, who was the first person PJ's age to read a draft of the work and whose enthusiasm spurred me to develop the characters. I am equally grateful for the sharp feedback from Cici Todeschini (Rome), Angela Neustatter (London), Gary Smith (Toronto), Deborah Lyons, PhD (Austin), and Teri Rodriguez (Austin).

Finally I thank my dear neighbor Tina Huckabee for her friendship and comments as she read the work chapter by chapter. We all mourned the death of her daughter Shoshana Weintraub (1992–2006), who gave so much of herself to our community. Part of the proceeds of *Sunshine Picklelime* will be donated to Austin's Town Lake Animal Center in Shoshana's memory, to honor the years she volunteered there, along with Tina and Steve and Aaron Weintraub.

about the author

Only a person who has lived as richly as Pamela Ellen Ferguson could create such a lush work of fiction. She was born in Mexico, grew up in Britain and South Africa, and has lived and worked in over a dozen world capitals. A former journalist in London's Fleet Street, she is now an award-winning international instructor in Zen Shiatsu, and her books for adults, both fiction and non-fiction, have been translated into several languages. She lives in Austin, Texas, surrounded by a garden with cacti as tall as trees. *Sunshine Picklelime* is her first book for children.